John L. Stoddard

John L. Stoddard's Lectures

illustrated and embellished with views of the world's famous places and people,

being the identical discourses delivered during the past eighteen years under the

title of the Stoddard lectures - Vol. 1

John L. Stoddard

John L. Stoddard's Lectures
illustrated and embellished with views of the world's famous places and people, being the identical discourses delivered during the past eighteen years under the title of the Stoddard lectures - Vol. 1

ISBN/EAN: 9783337399535

Printed in Europe, USA, Canada, Australia, Japan

Cover: Foto ©Andreas Hilbeck / pixelio.de

More available books at **www.hansebooks.com**

JOHN L. STODDARD'S LECTURES

ILLUSTRATED AND EMBELLISHED WITH VIEWS OF THE
WORLD'S FAMOUS PLACES AND PEOPLE, BEING
THE IDENTICAL DISCOURSES DELIVERED
DURING THE PAST EIGHTEEN
YEARS UNDER THE TITLE
OF THE STODDARD
LECTURES

COMPLETE IN TEN VOLUMES

VOLUME I

BOSTON
BALCH BROTHERS CO.
MDCCCXCVIII
CHICAGO: GEO. L. SHUMAN & CO.

JOHN L. STODDARD was born in Brookline, Mass., April 24, 1850. He graduated at Williams College, as valedictorian of his class, in 1871, and then studied theology for two years at Yale Divinity School. Next he taught Latin and French in the Boston Latin School. In 1874 he was able to gratify a long cherished desire to travel in foreign lands, and not only made the customary tour of Europe, but visited Greece, Asia Minor, Palestine and Egypt as well. He then studied in Germany, and upon his return to America, began his career as a lecturer, which for about twenty years has known no interruptions save those due to his repeated visits to remote countries. His travels embrace nearly all the habitable parts of the globe.

John L. Stoddard.

PREFACE

A WITTY French abbé was once asked why he kept up a country-seat which he never visited. "Do you not know," he answered, "that I must have some place, where, though I never go to it, I can always imagine that I might be happier than where I am?" The world is like the abbé. Most of us are not living, we are anticipating life. We are always "going to our country seats." It is the land we have not visited that is to give to us our greatest happiness. If we have not yet found it in America, it is awaiting us in Europe; if not in Europe, surely in Japan. As the Germans say, "Da wo ich nicht bin, da ist das Glück." Hence travel is attractive, if only as a means of acquiring that happiness which here seems so elusive. All of us hope to some day visit Europe and the Orient, and for that reason everything pertaining to their beauty, art, and history seems alluring. But when these have been seen, the wished-for goal of the untraveled world again recedes, and the desire is just as strong to visit other and more distant lands.

This love of travel is not caused by ordinary restlessness. It springs originally from the universal craving of the soul for something different from its usual environment.

It also comes from a legitimate longing for that broader education which only personal study of other races, civilizations and religions can bestow. And, finally, it arises from a yearning for the joy and benefit of *realizing history* by visiting the ancient shrines of art, the homes or sepulchres of heroes, and the arenas of heroic deeds. When such desires are once awakened, to travel is to live, to remain continually in one place is to stagnate.

Thousands of books of travel have been written, but notwithstanding that the scenes described in them are practically the same, and though the streets and buildings which adorn their text are perfectly familiar to their readers, such works are usually welcome, and always in proportion to the degree in which mere figures and statistics are subordinated to the *ideas* suggested by such travel to the writer's mind, which, of course, vary infinitely according to the culture, sympathy and enthusiasm of the individual.   Thus, in a similar way, the keys of all pianos are the same; yet it is not the bits of ivory themselves that hold us spell-bound, but the magnetic fingers that move over them, and the musical interpretation and expression given by the performer.

If only accurate statistics and detailed descriptions were desired, guide-books would be sufficient; but who ever reads a guide-book for amusement?

Such thoughts have encouraged the author of these volumes to present in printed form lectures which for eighteen years have been received with never-failing kindness by an indulgent public.   *Verba volant; Scripta manent* (Words are fleeting, but what is written remains).   The voice of the speaker dies away, and what he says is soon forgotten, but on these printed pages, that which has really caused whatever success the "Stoddard Lectures" have achieved, may be recalled precisely as the lectures were heard, accompanied too by even more embellishment than illustrated them at the time of their delivery.   It has always given the writer a singular sensation to meet his audiences season after season after the separation of a year.   Were they the same individuals whom he had last addressed?   He could not tell.   They could be absolutely sure of his identity, but he was quite unable to determine theirs.   Beyond the curve of platform or of stage, he could not distinguish the auditors of former years from those who were seated there for the first time. Sometimes they seemed to him scarcely more real and tangible than were the views that came and went so noiselessly upon the screen. He looked for a few moments at an amphitheatre of expectant faces, then darkness would transform them into rows of phantoms, and at the end he saw them rise and disappear, like a great fleet of ships that separates and scatters on a trackless sea.

In these volumes, however, he hopes to meet his audiences more frequently, and for a longer time than ever before. If, then, the oral lectures may have given the public some enjoyment in the past, it is the author's hope that when he himself no longer greets his former listeners, year by year, these souvenirs of travel may in this form find a more enduring place among the pleasures of their memories.

In that case he will not be utterly forgotten, for pleasant memories can never be taken from us; they are the only joys of which we can be absolutely sure.

John L. Stoddard.

NORWAY.

O F all the countries on our globe, Norway, in some respects, must rank as the most wonderful. From the North Cape to its most southern limit the distance is about eleven hundred miles. Nearly one-third of this great area lies within the Arctic circle. One would expect its climate to be that of Greenland; but Nature saves it, as a habitation for the race, by sending thither the mysterious Gulf Stream, which crosses the Atlantic for five thousand miles, and, although far spent on that distant shore, fulfills its mission, transforming, by its still warm breath, an otherwise barren region to a fertile land. But this is only the beginning of Norway's wonders. Exposed

KING OSCAR II.

to all the fury of the North Sea, Arctic and Atlantic, the navigation of its coast would be well-nigh impossible had not indulgent Nature made here countless breakwaters, by means of a vast fringe of islands more than a thousand miles in length, behind which are smooth, sheltered channels for the largest ships.

Again, Norwegian mountains come directly to the sea. On this account, one might suppose that the interior would be inaccessible. But Nature does here one more act of kindness, and penetrates these mountain walls at many points with ocean avenues, sometimes a hundred miles in length, and with such depth that, at their farthest limits, steamers may come directly to the shore. Moreover, to enhance its mystery and beauty, Nature bestows on this, her favorite, a day that is a summer long, — a light that never elsewhere was on land or sea, — and makes its splendid vistas still more glorious by a midnight sun.

There have been

THE HARBOR OF CHRISTIANIA.

few experiences in my life more joyous and exhilarating than my arrival in Christiania. It was six o'clock in the morning as our steamer glided up its noble harbor. The sky was cloudless; the water of the deepest blue; a few white sails rose here and there, like sea-gulls, from the waves. The forest-covered islands, emerald to the water's edge, seemed gems upon the bosom of the bay. Beyond, were mountains glistening in an atmosphere, the like of which, for clearness, I had never seen: while the first breath of that crisp, aromatic air (a most delicious blending of the odors of mountain, sea, and forest) can never be forgotten.

"This, this is Norway!" we exclaimed, "and it is all before us; first, in the joy of exploration; then in the calmer, though perpetual, pleasure of its retrospection."

Excited by our anticipations, we disembarked as

THE VICTORIA HOTEL.

speedily as possible, and hastened to the Hotel Victoria. It is a well-kept, comfortable hostelry, whose chief peculiarity is a spacious courtyard, where frequently, in summer, *table d'hôte* is served beneath a mammoth tent of gorgeous colors. Moreover, it is a pleasant rendezvous for travelers; for while some tourists are here setting forth upon their inland journey, others have just completed it, and with bronzed faces tell strange stories of the North, which sound like tales invented by Munchausen.

MR. BENNETT,
THE TRAVELER'S FRIEND.

Impatient to arrange our route, after a breakfast in the hotel courtyard we went directly to the individual known as "Bennett." "Bennett? Who is Bennett?" the reader perhaps exclaims. My friend, there is but one Norway, and Bennett is its prophet. Bennett is the living encyclopædia of Norway;

its animated map; its peripatetic guide-book. Nor is this all. He is the traveler's guide, philosopher, and friend. He sketches lengthy tours back and forth as easily as sailors box the compass; tells him which roads to take and which to avoid; sends word ahead for carriages and horses; engages rooms for him within the Arctic circle; forwards his letters, so that he may read them by the midnight sun; gives him a list of carriage-coupons which the coachmen cry for; and (more important still) so plans his

A NORTHERN LANDSCAPE.

numerous arrivals and departures on the coast that he may always find a train or steamer there awaiting him. This is a most essential thing in Norway.

As a rule, Norwegian time-tables are about as difficult to decipher as the inscriptions on a Chinese tea-caddy. Even Bradshaw, the author of that English railway guide which is the cause of so much apoplexy, came here to Norway a few years ago, and died in trying to make out its post-road and railway system. Some think that it was a judgment

IN NORWAY.

upon him.   At all events, his grave is near Christiania, and he
sleeps, while the "globe-trotter," whom he long befriended,
still rushes to and fro.

Although an Englishman by birth, "Bennett" has been
for fifty years a resident of Norway, and is a blessing to all
travelers in that country.   At first he gave his services gratu-
itously; but as the tourists began to multiply, he found that
such disinterestedness was impossible.   He at length made
a business of it, and year by year it has steadily increased.

A new edition of his guide-book comes out every season;
and to still further help the public, he has begotten four
young Bennetts, who act as courteous agents for their
father, in Bergen, Trondhjem, and Christiania.   He has

no "personally conducted
parties." He has no wish
to go outside of Norway.
But here, on account of
the peculiar style of traveling, and the difficulty of the
language, it certainly is a
great convenience to employ
him.

Our arrangements with
this guardian of Norwegian
tourists having at length
been concluded, we strolled
for some time through Christiania's streets.   It is a clean
and cheerful city, though it
can boast of little architectural beauty.   The Royal
Palace is its finest building,
but even this, on close inspection, proves to be more

CHRISTIANIA FJORD.

THE PALACE AT CHRISTIANIA.

useful than or-
namental, and
well suited to a
nation forced to
practice strict
economy. In
inspecting the
structure it is
interesting to
remember how
independent
Norway is of Sweden, although both countries are governed
by one King. The Parliament in Christiania is wholly separate from that of Stockholm. No Swede may hold political
office here. Even the power of the King is limited; for
if a bill is passed three times in the Norwegian Parliament,
then, notwithstanding the royal veto, it becomes law.

Moreover, in accordance with the Constitution, the King
of Sweden and Norway must be crowned in Norway; he must
reside here three months in the year; here, also, he must
open Parliament in person, and hold receptions, for no Norwegian wishes to go to Stockholm for a presentation to
his sovereign. In this portion of his realm, also, he must
be addressed as " King of Norway and Sweden," not of
" Sweden and Norway." A
certain rival-ry still exists be-tween
these two

nations. Norwegians sometimes say: "We love the English, and drink tea; the Swedes love the French, and drink coffee!"

One of the first things that attracted my attention in my walks through Christiania was the peculiar sign, "Rum för

AN AMBIGUOUS SIGN.

Resande." Judge not, however, from appearances in this strange language of the north. It is said that not long ago an English-speaking traveler of strong prohibition principles was horrified at seeing this announcement frequently displayed.

"What does that last word 'Resande' mean?" he asked suspiciously.

"Travelers," was the reply.

"Rum for travelers!" he exclaimed. "Oh, this is terrible! What an insult to the traveling public! Now I, for one, protest against such misrepresentation. I am a traveler, but I never take a drop of rum."

A BIT OF NORWAY.

LAKE MJÖSEN.

"Not quite so fast," rejoined a Norwegian, who was laughing heartily; "that first word means, not *rum*, but *rooms;* the whole sentence, therefore, merely signifies, 'lodging for travelers.'" Eager to start upon our northward journey, we left some interesting features in Christiania for a later visit, and on a beautiful June morning set out for the coast. The train conveyed us in two hours to Lake Mjösen, where we embarked upon a little steamer. From that time on, although continually traveling, we saw no more railways for a month. This lovely sheet of water has a marvelous depth, its bed, in places, being one thousand feet below the level of the sea. This fact grows more mysterious when we remember that on the occasion of the Lisbon earthquake, in 1755, the waters of this lake, although so remote from Portugal, were so terribly disturbed, that they rose suddenly to the height of twenty

A WISE CAPTAIN.

feet, and then as suddenly subsided.

It was while sailing on the waters of Lake Mjösen that we had another curious linguistic experience. Next to Norwegian or Swedish, English is best understood and spoken

A LANDING PIER.

by the natives, especially among the seafaring population. We did not know this fact at first, and as we had just come from Germany, it seemed more natural to address the people in the Teutonic tongue. You know the German word for bright or clear is "hell." Accordingly, desiring to ask the captain if he thought that the weather would be fine, my friend

stepped up to him, and pointing to the sky, said interrogatively, "Hell?"

"No," replied the captain, in perfectly good English, "hell doesn't lie in that direction!"

A sail of several hours here through charming scenery brought us at last to the place where we were to disembark. Hardly had I set foot upon the pier, when a man accosted me in good, familiar English:

"Just step this way, sir, if you please," he said; "the carriage ordered for you by Mr. Bennett is all ready."

This surely was a pleasant introduction. There was no trouble whatsoever — no bargaining, no delay. In fifteen minutes we had started on our four days' journey to the sea.

Between Christiania and the western coast is a broad mountain range extending hundreds of miles north and south.

A LOVELY DRIVE.

No railroad crosses that gigantic barrier. True, the town of Trondhjem, in the north, can now be reached circuitously by rail. But all the great southwestern coast, including the towns of Bergen and Molde, and the large fjords, can only be approached by several magnificent highways, of which the finest here awaited us, the one extending for a hundred and sixty miles from Lake Mjosen to the Songe fjord. And here one naturally asks, "What is the mode of traveling in Norway? Where do you eat? Where do you sleep? Do you take horses for the entire

SÆTERSDALEN.

journey, or from day to day?" It is easily explained. All these Norwegian highways are divided into sections, each about ten miles long. These sections have at one extremity a "station" (usually a farmhouse), the owner of which is obliged by law to give to travelers food and lodging, and also to supply them with fresh horses to the next station.

FINE NORWEGIAN STATION.

These Norwegian posthouses are invariably made of wood, sometimes elaborately carved and decorated. As you approach the door, some member of the family greets you, frequently in English, since many of these people have been in America. If you desire to spend the night, you ask for rooms. If you merely require dinner, you can be quickly served; or if your purpose is to drive on still farther, you simply order fresh horses. For these we never waited more than fifteen minutes, though sometimes, in the height of the season, serious delays take place. On this account it is better to precede the crowd of tourists, and visit Norway early in the summer. Such has been my experience, at least; and judging from some stories I have heard of tourists sleeping on the floor and dressing on the back piazza, I should emphatically recommend this rule to all adventurers in the land of Thor.

A CARIOLE.

But speaking of Norwegian post-stations reminds one of the characteristic vehicle of Norway, —the cariole. This is by no means a "carry-all." It is a little gig, intended for only one person. True, the boy (or, in some instances, the girl) who takes the horse back after you have done with it, rides behind. His seat is your valise, and his weight determines the subsequent condition of its contents! There is a charming lightness in these carioles. The springs are good, and the seat is easy. A leather apron reaches to your waist to shield you from the dust or rain; and, drawn by a Norwegian pony, such a drive is wonderfully exhilarating.

These little carriages have, however, one great fault,— their want of sociability. The linguistic powers of a Norwegian post-boy are extremely limited; and when you have ridden ten hours a day, unable to exchange a word with your friends except by shouting, the drive becomes a trifle wearisome. But the reader may ask: "Is there not sometimes great discomfort in traveling by

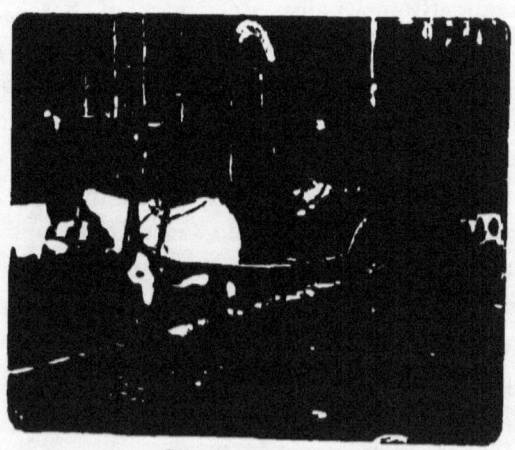

THE NATIONAL VEHICLE.

LUXURY IN NORWAY.

carioles in rainy weather?" Assuredly there is. But in such weather one is not obliged to take a cariole. Norway has other vehicles. We drove, for example, about a hundred and thirty miles in a sort of victoria, the rear of which could be entirely covered in case of rain. This, all in all, I hold to be the best conveyance for the tourist in Norway, especially when ladies are of the party. I know that such a carriage is considered too luxurious by the English; but I am sure that American ladies will gain more pleasure and profit from Norwegian travel if they do not attempt to drive all day in carioles; and if beneath the canopy provided they keep their clothing dry.

At home we would not think of driving forty miles a day in an open wagon through the rain; why, then, should we do it unnecessarily in Norway, where showers are proverbially both frequent and copious? As for the fun and novelty of cariole-riding, these can always be had, for several hours at a time, between one station and another, even if one has engaged a larger carriage for the entire journey, for the cost of a cariole and pony for half a day is ludicrously small, and the change to it, occasionally, well repays the slight expenditure.

A PEASANT GIRL.

But in thus speaking of the cariole, I have unwittingly put the cart before the horse. A word of praise must certainly be given to the usual Norwegian steed. Of all the ponies I have ever seen, these of Norway are at once the strongest,

A NORWEGIAN PONY.

prettiest, and most lovable. They are usually of a delicate cream color, with one dark line along the back, the mane being always closely cut. These ponies are employed in Norway almost universally, being not only less expensive but really more en-during than the larger horses. For weeks we drove behind these little animals, till we had test-ed certainly seventy-five

A FARM SCENE.

of them, and never once did we observe in any of them the slightest ugliness or a vicious trait. They are, moreover, wonderfully sure-footed. I never saw one stumble or go lame. Possibly, later in the season, when much over-worked, they may not have the spirit which we found in them; but in our drives of more than two hundred miles there was not one which did not cheerfully respond to any call.

This being premised, let us really begin our journey. At first we found the scenery more beautiful than grand. In many places I could have believed myself in portions of either of the American states of New Hampshire or Vermont. Across the fields I often noticed long, dark lines which, in the distance, looked like hedges. On examination, however, these proved to be wooden fences, covered with new - mown grass; for, in this way, Norwegian farmers "make hay while the sun shines." Some of these fences are very low, but others have considerable height. Norwegian farmers claim that grass hung thus, and thoroughly exposed to wind and sun, will shed the rain and dry more quickly than if left upon the ground.

A MAUD MULLER.

Their theory seems reasonable, and the extent of the hay crop, which is very important, further justifies it. There is one other argument in favor of these hay-racks, — during all other seasons of the year they serve as clothes-lines for the family washing. But even more peculiar than the fences were the vehicles used for hauling the hay into Norwegian barns. We laughed at first sight of these rustic carts. They are only a trifle larger than a good-sized cradle, and are perched upon the smallest wheels I ever

A HAY CART.

saw on anything except a toy. Yet there is good reason for their use, for on Norwegian farms the loads are drawn, not by stout oxen, but by little ponies. Moreover, the grass is often cut from the edge of precipices, or in deep ravines, and these low carts are certainly better adapted than high and heavy ones for locomotion in such regions.

While thus absorbed in agricultural reflections, we drove up to the house where we were to take supper. A pleasant-featured girl, with a baby in her arms, invited us to enter. She spoke English perfectly, having been born, as we learned, in Minneapolis.

AT A FARM HOUSE.

I shall never forget that first Norwegian supper. The name for the evening meal in Norway is "aftenmad," but *oftenmad* would better express it in English. First, there were placed before us five different kinds of cheese, the most remarkable of which was a tall monument of chocolate-colored substance made from goat's milk. This, by Norwegians, is considered perfectly delicious; but for a month I shuddered at it regularly three times a day. Next was brought in a jar containing fish. At this my friend smiled joyfully.

A NORWEGIAN HAY-FIELD.

"Ah," he exclaimed, "here is fish! Anything in the line of fish I can eat with a relish."

He drew a specimen from the jar, and put a portion of it in his mouth. A look of horror instantly overspread his face, and, covering his features with a napkin, he left the room in haste. I quickly followed him, and found him in the back yard gazing mournfully at some Norwegian swine.

"What is the matter?" I asked, "do you prefer pork to fish?"

"I believe I do," he rejoined. Then turning to the girl, who had followed us, he inquired, "What is the Norwegian word for pork?"

"DO YOU PREFER PORK TO FISH?"

"Griss,"* was the reply.

"Thank you," he faltered, "I don't think I will take any to-day."

"Eh" (in an aside to me), "had n't we better drive on?"

"Drive on?" I cried. "Drive on, when there is plenty of fish, which you always eat with so much relish?"

"Great heavens!" he groaned, "that was too much even for me. It was a raw anchovy dipped in vinegar."

While this colloquy was taking place, we re-entered the dining-room and asked for bread. We were amazed to see what this request brought forth. Upon a plate almost as large as the wheel of a Norwegian hay-cart was brought to us a mound of circular wafers nearly three feet in circumference, and each about as thick as one of our buckwheat cakes.

* Pronounced as is our English word *grease*.

NORWEGIAN PEASANTS.

They were made of rye meal and water (chiefly water), and
were so crisp that they would break to pieces at a touch.
This is called "flatbrod," and it is certainly in every sense the
flattest article ever invented for the human stomach. The
people, however, are fond of it, and I saw horses eat it frequently, mistaking it (quite naturally, I am sure) for tablets
of compressed hay.

But here I shall probably be asked, "Is this the usual
state of things in Norway?" No, this first station was
unusually poor. The staple article of food in Norway
(always fresh and good) is salmon. Milk and sweet butter
can also be had, and eggs *ad libitum*. In fact, the abund-
ance of eggs here is probably responsible for the atrocious
witticism often perpetrated by Norwegian tourists, to the
effect that "if the sun does not set in Norway, hens do."
Mutton and beef are not obtainable, save at the large hotels,
their places being usually supplied by veal, sausage meat,
or reindeer hash. I met, while traveling here, an Englishman,
who said to me, "I did intend to drive on to Christiania;

NORWAY SCENERY.

but I really can't, you know; another month of this would kill me. In the last two weeks I have eaten so many of these 'blasted eggs' that I 'm ashamed to look a hen in the face!'' Yet, notwithstanding the hardships which the traveler meets in Norway in regard to food, he will find all discomforts

easily outweighed by the enjoyment of the trip. The constant exercise in the open air gives powers of digestion hitherto unknown, preceded by an appetite which laughs at everything, ... save cheese. Of course, being so

A TRAVELER'S PARADISE.

far from any city, one cannot look for luxuries at these small stations; indeed, I was surprised to find that the peasants knew enough to give us, during a meal, several knives and forks, hot plates, and other features of a well-served table. And as far as prices are concerned, they are so moderate as to provoke a smile from any one accustomed to travel in other parts of Europe.

Yes, all ordinary discomforts sink into insignificance, as I recall those memorable drives, day after day and hour after hour, over lofty mountains, through noble forests, and beside stupendous cliffs, the only sounds about us being the songs of birds and the perpetual melody of numberless cascades. Moreover, this mode of travel gave us the energy

of athletes. For how can I describe the invigoration and
sweetness of the air of Norway, — pure from its miles of
mountains, — rich with the fragrance of a billion pines, and
freshened by its passage over northern glaciers and the Arctic
sea?

As for Norwegian roads, they are among the finest in the
world. The majority of them are flanked with telegraph-poles;
for not only are these routes magnificent specimens of man's
triumph over nature, but the lightning also is controlled here,
and, swift as light, thought wings its way upon a metal wire through this inland waste, — a marvel always wonderful and ever new. Nature has given to these scenes the trees and rocks which yield to nothing but the wintry blasts. Man has suspended

A NORWEGIAN HIGHWAY.

here a thread of steel, which thrills responsive to the thoughts
of thousands, transmitting through the gloomiest gorges the
messages of love, hope, exultation, or despair. Hence one can
never feel completely isolated here. That little wire enables
him at any point to vanquish space, and by placing, as it were,
a finger on the pulse of life, to feel the heart-beats of the
world.

In 1888, two American gentlemen were traveling in Norway,

one of whom grew depressed at his apparent isolation from humanity. His comrade, to astonish and console him, telegraphed from one of the post-houses where they had stopped for dinner, to the American consul at Christiania. The message which he sent was this:

APPARENT ISOLATION.

"Who was the Democratic nominee for President yesterday in Chicago?"

Before the meal was finished, the answer had arrived:

"Grover Cleveland."

Some of the roads on which we traveled here are cut directly through the mountains. We found such tunnels quite agreeable, since they furnished the only genuine darkness to be found. So far as light is concerned, one may drive through Norway in the summer just as well by night as by day. Early and late indeed are words which in this region grow meaningless. I could not keep a diary in Norway, so difficult was it to tell when yesterday ended and to-day

began.   At first this seemed a great economy of time.   We
felt that we were getting some advantage over Mother
Nature.   "Why not drive on another twenty miles?" we
asked; "we can enjoy the scenery just as well;" or, "Why
not write a few   letters now? It
is still light.   In fact, why
go to bed   at all?"
But   after

a time
this everlast-
ing daylight grew
a trifle wearisome.   A LAND OF PERPETUAL SUNLIGHT.

It thoroughly demoralized both our brains and our stomachs,
from the unheard of hours it occasioned for eating and
sleeping.   Steamers will start in Norway at five o'clock
in the morning, or even at midnight.   I once sat down
to a *table d'hôte* dinner at half-past nine, and on another
occasion ate a lunch in broad daylight at two o'clock in the
morning.   Moreover, even when we went to bed the sun's

NORWEGIAN BOULDERS.

rays stole between our eyelids, and dispelled that darkness which induces slumber. For, strangely enough, there are rarely any blinds or shutters to Norwegian windows. Only a thin, white curtain screened us usually from the glare of day. After a while, therefore, I could sympathize with an American lady, whom I heard

DISINTEGRATED MOUNTAINS.

exclaim, "O, I would give anything for a good, pitch-dark night twenty-four hours long!"

One characteristic of these roads made on my mind a profound impression, namely, the boulders that have been split off from overhanging peaks by frost and avalanche. This is a feature of Norwegian scenery that I have never seen equaled in the world. Sometimes we drove through such *débris* for half an hour. Nor is there the least exaggeration in the statement that these boulders are in many instances as large as a house; yet, when compared with the gigantic cliffs from which they came, even such monsters

A NORWAY PRECIPICE.

seemed like pebbles. Some of these cliffs were frightful in appearance. Again and again, when we had passed beneath some precipice, one third of whose mass seemed only waiting for a thunder-peal to bring it down, my friend and I would draw a long, deep breath, and exchange glances of congratu-

A CHARACTERISTIC CASCADE.

lation when we had escaped its terrors.

A still more wonderful feature of Norwegian scenery is found in its imposing waterfalls. Nothing in Norway so astonished me as the unending number and variety of its cascades, — ribbons of silver, usually, in the distance, but foaming torrents close at hand. On any of these roads, halt for a moment and listen, and you will often hear a sound like that of the surf upon the shore. It is the voice of falling water.

On our journey toward the coast, during a drive of three days we counted one hundred and sixty separate falls, and eighty - six in the previous ten hours. This was an average of more than two in every fifteen minutes. True, we saw

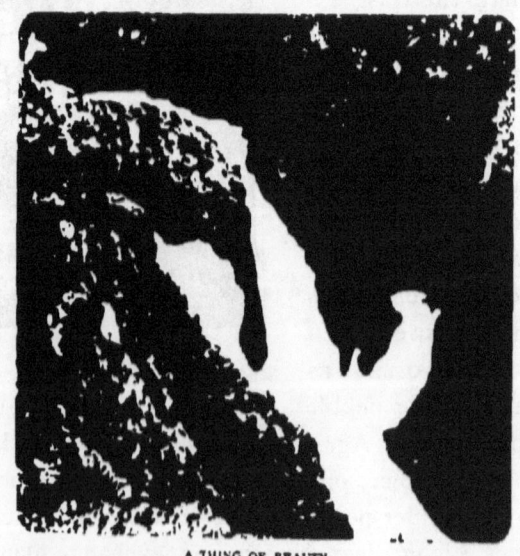

A THING OF BEAUTY.

VIEW NEAR BORGUND.

these cascades in the month of June, when snow was melting rapidly on the heights; but even in midsummer they must far outnumber those in any other part of Europe.

In fact, although familiar with the Alps, and having driven twice through all the valleys of the Pyrenees, I never knew how many waterfalls one country could possess until I went to Norway. There are, of course, magnificent falls in Switzerland, and a great number of them in the Pyrenees; but where you there see one cascade, in Norway you see twenty; and many a Norwegian cataract which would in Switzerland draw thousands of admiring tourists, and make the fortune of hotel proprietors, is here, perhaps, without a name, and certainly without renown.

BORGUND CHURCH.

On our last day's journey toward the sea, we came in sight of an extraordinary building, on which we gazed in great astonishment, for it seemed more appropriate to China than to Norway, and was apparently completely out of place in this wild, desolate ravine. It was the famous Borgund Church, a place of early Christian worship, built about eight hundred years ago. It therefore ranks (unless one other similar church be excepted) as the oldest structure in all Norway. It is so small that one could almost fancy it a church for dwarfs. Around the base is a kind of cloister, from which the dim interior receives its only light. Within is one small room,

A GIRL OF NORWAY.

scarcely forty feet long, containing now no furniture save a rough-hewn altar. As for its various roofs and pinnacles, marked now by crosses, now by dragons' heads, nothing could be more weirdly picturesque, especially as the entire edifice is black, — in part from age, but chiefly from the coats of tar with which it has been painted for protection.

Leaving this ancient church, we soon found ourselves in one of the most stupendous of Norwegian gorges. It is hardly possible for any view to do it justice. But for awe-inspiring grandeur I have never seen its magnificence surpassed, even in the Via Mala. For miles the river Laerdal makes its way here through gigantic cliffs, which rise on either side to a height of from four thousand to five thousand feet. The space, however, between these mountain sides is barely wide enough for the river, which writhes and struggles with obstructing boulders, lashing itself to creamy foam, and filling the chasm with a deafening roar. Yet, above the river, a roadway

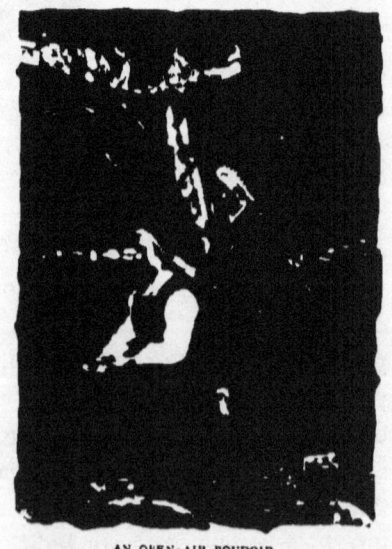

AN OPEN-AIR BOUDOIR.

SELTUNSAASEN IN LAERDAL.

has been hewn
out of the moun-
tain-side itself,
which is lined
with parapets of
boulders. When
marking out the
route the engi-
neers were often
lowered over

A LANDING PLACE.

the precipice by ropes.   One can imagine nothing more
exciting than this drive.   When mountains did not actually
overshadow us, in looking aloft we could discern only a
narrow rift of sky, like a blue river, curbed by granite banks.
Below us was the seething flood, at once terrible and glorious to look upon.   Shut in by these huge, somber walls, we
followed all the windings of the stream, whirling about their
corners at a speed which seemed the more terrific from our
wild surroundings.   There are few things in life that have
affected me so powerfully as the Laerdal gorge, and I would
once more go to Norway for that drive alone.   Certain it is
that at the end of it we found ourselves exhausted, not phy-
sically, but nervously, from the tremendous tension and
excitement of the last few hours in this wild ravine.   Finally,

LAERDALSÖREN.

leaving this sublime mountain scenery, we saw between us
and the coast our destination — the little town of Laerdalsören. Thrilled though we were with memories of what we
had just seen, and grateful, too, that our long drive from
sea to sea had been successfully completed, our serious
reflections vanished at the threshold of this village. My
companion had found it hard to be so long deprived of
news from home. Accordingly, he remarked to me as we
came in sight of Laerdalsören:

"I somehow feel to-day a great anxiety about my boys,
William and Henry. I am not superstitious, but I have
a presentiment that they need me. Hark!" he said suddenly, "what 's that?"

We stopped the vehicle and listened. It was the music
of an English hand-organ; and I am speaking only the literal
truth when I say that the tune which we then heard it play
was that of "Father, dear father, come home with me now."

WAITING FOR TOURISTS.

Early next morning we left our good hotel and hastened
to the steamer which awaited us upon the fjord. "What,
precisely, is a fjord?" some may inquire. In briefest terms,
it is a mountain gorge connected with the ocean, a narrow
arm of the sea extending inland, sometimes for one hundred
miles. Moreover, to carry out the simile, at the extremity of
every such long
arm are "fin-
gers;" that is,
still narrower ex-
tensions, which
wind about the
bases of the
mountains till
they seem like
glittering ser-
pents lying in
the shadow of
tremendous
cliffs.

Thus in one
sense, here at

A FJORD.

Laerdalsören, we had reached the sea, but in another, it
was still eighty-five miles away. Yet we were now to
embark on a large ocean steamer, lying but a few yards
from the shore, for these mysterious fjords are sometimes
quite as deep as the mountains over them are high. They
open thus the very heart of Norway to the commerce
of the world. And as our steamer glided from one moun-
tain-girdled basin into another, I realized why this western
coast of Norway is one of the most remarkable land-forma-
tions on the globe. If we were able to look down upon it
from an elevation, we should perceive that from the mountain chain, which forms, as it were, the backbone of the coun-

try, a multitude of grooves stretch downward to the shore
between the elevations, like spaces between the teeth of a comb.
Into these mountain crevices, formed in the misty ages of the
past, the sea now makes its way, continually growing narrower,
until at last it winds between frowning cliffs of fearful height,
down which stream numerous waterfalls, the spray from which
at times sweeps
over the steamer
as it glides along.
Traveling, there-
fore, on these
ocean avenues
is like sailing

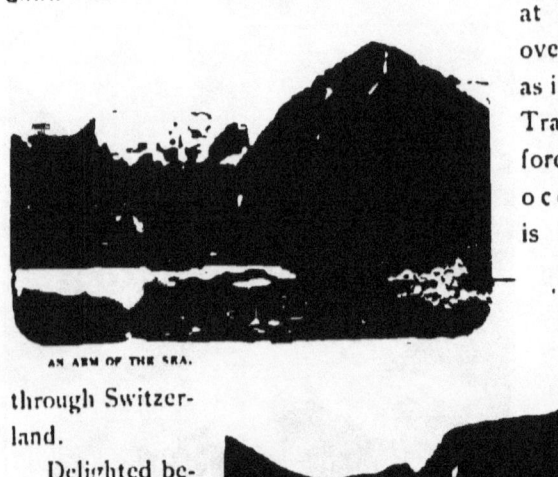

AN ARM OF THE SEA.

through Switzer-
land.

Delighted be-
yond measure
with this new ex-
perience, some
two or three
hours after leav-

SAILING THROUGH SWITZERLAND.

ing Laerdalsören, we gradually approached the most sublime
of all these ocean highways, — the Naerofjord. No general
view can possibly portray its grandeur. The only way to
appreciate the vastness of its well-nigh perpendicular cliffs
is to compare them with some objects on the banks. In
many places, for example, cattle grazing on the shore, compared with their giant environment, seemed like mice, and a
church steeple appeared no larger than a pine-cone.

As we sailed further up this beautiful expanse, it was
difficult to realize that we were floating on an arm of the

THE NAEROFJORD.

Atlantic. It had the appearance rather of a gloomy lake shut in by mountains never trodden by the foot of man. On either side was a solemn array of stupendous precipices — sheer, awful cliffs — refusing even the companionship of pines and hemlocks, and frequently resembling a long chain of icebergs turned to stone. The silence, too, was most impressive. There was, at times, no sign of life on sea or shore. The influence of this was felt upon the boat, for if any of us spoke, it was in a tone subdued by the solemnity of our surroundings.

As we pursued our way, sometimes we could discern no outlet whatever; then, suddenly, our course would turn, and

CONTINUALLY GROWING NARROWER.

another glorious vista would appear before us. We sat at the prow of the boat; and there, with nothing but the awe-inspiring prospect to contemplate, we sailed along in silence through this liquid labyrinth. So close together were the cliffs, that when, for the sake of the experiment, I lay down on the deck and looked directly upward, I could at the same instant see both sides of the fjord cutting their outlines sharply on the sky! Mile after mile, these grim, divided mountains stood gazing into each other's scowling faces, yet kept apart by this enchanting barrier of the sea, as some fair woman intervenes between two opposing rivals, each thirsting for the other's blood. It is such scenery as Dante might describe and Doré illustrate. We wondered what such ravines would look like without water.

They would be terrible to gaze

WALLS OF A FJORD.

upon. They would resemble gashes in a dead man's face, or chasms on the surface of the moon, devoid of atmosphere and life. But water gives to them vitality, and lights up all their gloomy gorges with a silvery flood, much as a smile illumines, while it softens, a furrowed face.

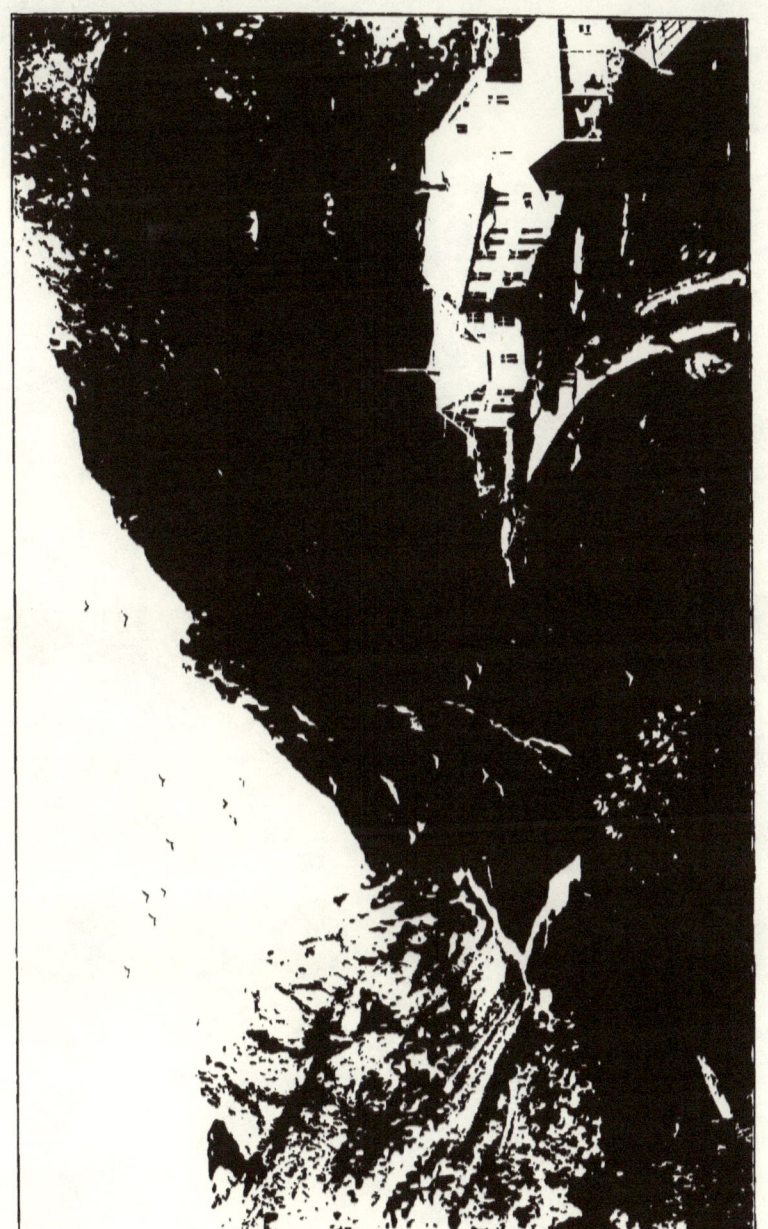

NÆRÖ VALLEY.

HEIGHTS AND DEPTHS.

Nor is the water in these fjords less marvelous than the land. Its depth, in places, is estimated at three thousand feet. When we sailed up the Naerofjord, its color was so green, and its surface so completely motionless, that we seemed to be gliding over a highway paved with malachite. Whether the coloring of these ocean avenues is due to their great depth, to the crystal clearness of the atmosphere, or to the reflection of the forests on their banks, certain it is that I have nowhere else (save in the blue grotto at Capri) seen water tinted with such shades of robin's-egg blue and emerald green. In confirmation of this fact,

AN OCEAN AVENUE.

we noticed with astonishment
that whenever the white seagulls,
wheeling round our boat, would
sink breast downward toward
the waves, the color of the sea
was so intense, that their white
wings distinctly changed their
hue in the reflected light, assum-
ing a most delicate tint, which
gradually vanished as they rose
again!

After a sail of several hours,
we approached the terminus of
the Naerofjord, at which is located the little hamlet of Gudvangen.   So narrow is the valley
here, that through the winter
months no ray of sunlight falls
directly on the town, and even in
the longest day in summer it can
receive the sunshine only for a
few hours.   It seemed depressing
to remain in such eternal shadow.
Accordingly, we halted only a
few moments at the place, and
taking a carriage which awaited
us, we drove beyond the village
into the ravine so celebrated for
its grandeur—the Naerodal. One
sees at once that this is really a
continuation of the Naerofjord
without the water. There can
be little doubt that, formerly, the
ocean entered it, and one could

A SUBLIME WATERFALL.

FJORD SCENERY.

then have sailed where we now had to drive. And what is true of the Nacrodal is also true of other such ravines. In every case the grooved hollows continue inland and upward, but the gradual elevation of the coast has caused the ocean to retreat. This is a place of great sublimity. On either side rise mountains from four to five thousand feet in height — sometimes without a vestige of vegetation on their precipitous sides — which are, however, seamed with numberless cascades, apparently hung upon the cliffs like silver chains.

The most remarkable object in the valley we found to be a peculiarly shaped mountain, called the Jordalsnut. Its form is that of

THE NAERODAL.

a gigantic thimble, and as its composition is a silvery feldspar, it fairly glitters in the sun, or glows resplendent in the evening light, — an object never to be forgotten. Those who have looked upon this dome by moonlight say that the effect is indescribable; and, in fact, moonlight in these awful gorges and fjords must give to them a beauty even more weird and startling than that of day. Of this, however, I cannot speak from experience, since moonlight is in summer very faint in Norway, and it is only earlier or later in the year that one can see this wonderful country thus transfigured.

In driving up the Naerodal, one sees, at the head of the valley, what looks like an irregular chalk-line on a blackboard. It is a famous carriage-road, which has been blasted out of the mountain-side, and built up everywhere with solid masonry. Even now it is so difficult of ascent for horses that every trav-

THE JOKDALSNUT.

eler who is able usually climbs that curving road on foot.

In doing so, we stopped at intervals to enjoy the marvelous scenery, and especially to behold the two attractive features of the mountain. For this grand terminus of the Naerodal is flanked on either side by a magnificent waterfall; and since the path continually curves, one or the other of these torrents is constantly visible. Either of them is the equal of any Swiss cascade I ever saw, and makes even the famous Giessbach sink into insignificance, and yet these are not ranked among the best Norwegian specimens. We could not, however, appreciate them as we should have done if they had been the first that we had seen; for when a tourist has counted eighty-six cascades in one day's drive, and has just run the gauntlet of some twenty more, in sailing through the Naerofjord, he becomes sur-feited with such splendor, and cannot properly realize what a glorious wealth in this respect Norwegian scen-ery possesses.

STALHEIM.

Upon the summit of the wooded cliff toward which this driveway leads, is a speck which at a distance resembles a white flag out-lined on the forest background. It is the Hotel Stalheim. As we approached it, a man stepped up to us and exclaimed:

THE VIEW FROM STALHEIM.

"Hullo, strang-ers; are you Americans?"

"I am glad to say that we are," was my reply.

He instantly stretched out his hand and said "Shake!"— "What kind of business are you in?" he present-ly inquired.

THE KAISER AT STALHEIM.

We told him.

"Well," he remarked, "I'm a manufacturer of barrel hoops. Norway's all right. I took an order for forty thousand yesterday."

At the dinner table, where he had greatly amused every one by his stories, he suddenly called out: "Waiter, is there anything worth seeing on that 'ere road down there?"

"It is one of the finest drives in Norway, sir," replied the waiter.

"Well, I reckon I'll have to do it, then," he ejaculated; and soon after dinner he departed in a cariole. An hour later, as I was sitting on the piazza gazing on the glorious prospect, I saw him coming back. "How is this?" I exclaimed; "I thought you were going to Gudvangen."

A SCENE NEAR STALHEIM.

A LOVELY CASCADE.

"No," he replied; "I got down here a piece, and met a boy. 'Bub,' says I, 'what is there to see down here, anyway?'

"'Waterfalls,' said he.

"'Waterfalls!' says I, 'I don't want any more waterfalls. I've seen ten thousand of them already. Why, our Niagara would n't roar one mite louder, if the whole lot of these Norwegian falls were chucked right into it.'"

I must not fail to add that there was an extremely pretty girl at the hotel, to whom our eccentric compatriot paid much attention. Some English travelers, therefore, looked greatly puzzled when they heard him say to her on taking leave: "Good-by! I hope *I'll strike you* again somewhere on the road!"

After supper that evening we took an extended walk. It was eleven o'clock, and yet the snow-capped mountains which surrounded us were radiant with the sunset glow. We presently encountered two young peasants returning from their

"GATES AJAR."

work. To them we spoke a few Norsk words that we had learned since coming to Norway, whereupon one of the lads drew from his pocket a pamphlet and presented it to me with a polite bow. It proved to be a book of phrases, half-English and half-Norsk, designed to help Norwegian emigrants

on landing in America. Not knowing, however, what it was at first, I opened it and could hardly believe my eyes, when, in this lonely valley in the heart of Norway, and by the light of a midnight sun I read these

ALL READY TO "SHAKE HANDS."

words: "Wake up! Here we are in Chicago!" "Change cars for Omaha and the West!" "Don't lean out of the window, or you'll have your head knocked off!"

Both of these bright boys hoped the next summer to "wake up in Chicago." It is, in fact, the great desire of Norwegian youths to go to America, and some are brave enough to do so with a capital of only twenty-five dollars. Their knowledge of the United States is, of course, limited, but one place there is known to all of them. Again and again we were subjected to the following questions: "Are you English?"

"No."

"Americans?"

"Yes."

"CHICAGO?"

That was the place for them, evidently. New York is better than nothing, but Chicago is the El Dorado of the Scan-
dinavians, for to that place they usually buy through-tickets,
as to the doorway of the great Northwest.

Leaving the Hotel Stalheim, after a short stay, a glorious
drive awaited us down to the Hardanger Fjord. At frequent
intervals along this route we encountered gates designed to
keep the cattle within certain limits. Women and children
usually stood near-by to open them, expecting in return a
trifling payment. Yet when I offered them a coin, I was
sometimes surprised to see their hands still lingering near my

own. At first I thought
that they, like Oliver Twist,
were asking for more, but
presently I discovered that
they merely wished to shake
hands and say good-by, for
hand-shaking in Norway is
universal. If you bestow a
fee upon your cariole-boy,
your boot-black, or your
chambermaid, each will offer
his or her hand to you and
wish you a happy journey.
A pleasant custom, truly,
but, on the whole, it is ad-
visable for travelers in Nor-

A PEASANT'S COTTAGE.

way to wear gloves. I usually responded cheerfully to this
mode of salutation, though sometimes, when I saw what
kind of a hand the peasant "held,"—I "passed!"

As we drove on, we noticed here and there the houses of
the poorer farmers. They are invariably made of wood, and

some, constructed out of huge spruce logs, look as enduring as the hills that surround them. The roofs are covered first with pieces of birch-bark, laid on the logs like shingles. On these are placed two layers of sod — the upper one with its grassy surface toward the sky. This grass is sometimes mown for hay. Occasionally a homœopathic crop of grain

RURAL LIFE.

will grow here. In almost every case the top of the house looks like a flower-garden; and I once saw a bearded goat getting his breakfast on his master's roof.

Occasionally, a little distance from the house, we saw another smaller structure, built beside a river; for the water-power of Norway is made use of in some simple way by almost all the country people. Many a peasant has a tiny water-wheel which turns a grindstone, or even a mill, and thus his scythes are sharpened and his grain is ground on his own premises. Such farmers, therefore, are their own millers, and frequently their own blacksmiths, too, and they can shoe their ponies with considerable skill.

In traveling through Norway it is most interesting to observe how the people utilize every available portion of the land. Wire ropes extend from the valleys up the mountain

A NORWEGIAN YOUTH.

sides, and are used for letting down
bundles of compressed hay, after it has
been reaped, gathered, and packed on
some almost inaccessible plateau. On
elevations, where it seems well-nigh
impossible for man to gain a foothold,
people will scramble, at the hazard of
their lives, to win a living from the
little earth that has there found lodg-
ment. Seeing with our own eyes these
habitable eyries, we could well believe
what we were told, that goats, and even
children, are often tied for safety to the
door-posts, and that the members of a
family who die on such elevated farms

A BEAST OF BURDEN.

are sometimes lowered by ropes a thousand feet down to the
valley or fjord.

It was on this journey that I took my first and never-to-
be-forgotten cariole-ride in Norway.
On this occasion, my driver was a
small boy, ten years old, just young
and mischievous enough to laugh at
danger and be reckless. I noticed
that his mother cautioned him before we started. She evidently
understood him. I did not. Accordingly, while I took the reins, I
gave him the whip. Springing like
a monkey into his place behind me,
he cracked his whip and off we
went. The road was good, and for
half an hour I thoroughly enjoyed
it. Then we began to descend,
and suddenly dashed across a bridge

A FISHING STATION.

beneath which was a foaming cataract. I naturally reined the pony in. But, to my surprise, the more I pulled, the faster went the pony. "Whoa!" I exclaimed; "whoa!" but whether prolonged or uttered with staccato emphasis that word made no apparent difference in the pony's gait. "Whoa," was evidently not in its vocabulary. My hair

THE SCENE OF AN ADVENTURE.

began to stand on end. Perceiving this, the demon of a boy commenced to utter the most unearthly yells, and to crack his whip until he made the pony actually seem to fly.

"Go slowly," I exclaimed. Crack, crack, went the whip.

"Stop that, you young rascal." Crack, crack, crack! I tried to seize the whip, but my tormentor held it far behind him. I sought to turn and petrify him with a look, but it was like trying to see a fly between my shoulder-blades. I saw that I was only making faces at the mountains.

To appreciate my feelings, one should perceive the winding road along which I was traveling. It was a splendid

specimen of en-
gineering skill,
but after twen-
ty-seven of
these curves, I
felt that I was
getting cross-
eyed. Fancy
me perched, as
it were, upon
a good-sized
salad-spoon,
flying around
the mountain
side, with one
wheel in the air

A CHARACTERISTIC LANDSCAPE.

at every turn, at the rate of the Chicago Limited going
round the Horse-shoe Bend. I looked back at my com-

ENGINEERING SKILL.

panion, whose
horse, excited
by my own,
was just behind
me. His face
was deathly
pale. Anxiety
was stamped
on every fea-
ture. His lips
moved as if
entreating me
to slacken this
terrific speed.
Finally, he
faintly cried:

"If you escape, . . . give my love . . . to my children, . . . William and Henry!"

At last I saw, some little way ahead, a cart half-blocking the road. "Great heavens!" I thought, " here comes a collision! Well, it might as well end this way as any other. No more lectures for me!" But, lo! there issued from the small boy's lips the sound, "Purr-r-r!" The effect was instantaneous. The horse at once relaxed his speed, and in a moment came to a full stop. For

A VIKING SHIP.

"purring" is to a Norwegian pony what the Westinghouse air-brake is to an express train. This secret learned, we had no further trouble. For "purr," when uttered by American lips, proved always as effectual as by Norwegian.

A few hours after that eventful ride, we found ourselves upon the great Hardangerfjord, which, with its branches, has a length of one hundred and forty miles. These ocean avenues possess not merely nat-ural beauty: they also have historic interest.

A LONELY POINT.

EIDFJORD IN HARDANGER—EXCURSION BOAT.

This part of Norway, for example, is old Viking ground. Not far from here lived Rollo, conqueror of Normandy; and from these fjords a thousand years ago went forth those dauntless warriors of the north, who for two hun-

AN ANCIENT BOAT OF NORWAY.

dred years not only ravaged England, France, and Ireland, but even crossed the Atlantic to America hundreds of years before Columbus sailed from Spain.

In this connection, therefore, let me say that, to me, the most interesting object in Christiania was its Viking ship. This most impressive relic of the past was found some fourteen years ago within an ancient mound beside the sea. It had reposed there for ten centuries, owing its preservation to the hard, blue clay in which it was entombed. It was made entirely of oak, and was propelled sometimes by oars, sometimes by a sail. Within it was discovered a well-carved wooden chair, in which, no doubt, the chieftain sat. Some kettles, too, were here,

and plates and drinking-cups, used by the Vikings when they
landed to prepare a meal. But, more remarkable still, this
boat contained some human bones. For in those early days
such boats were often used as funeral barges for their brave
commanders. The vessel, even when buried, was always
headed toward the sea, so that when called by Odin once
more into life, the chief whose body was thus sepulchered
might be ready to start at once and sail again the ocean he
had loved so well.

Occasionally, however, a Viking had a grander form of
burial. Sometimes, when an old Norwegian chieftain felt
that he was dying, he ordered that his body, when lifeless,
should be placed within his boat, which was then filled with
light materials and set on fire. The large sail was then spread,
and the dead warrior drifted out before the wind, his gallant
vessel for a funeral pyre, and for his liturgy the chanting of
the waves. As for the Viking himself, he doubtless had faced
death, sustained by an unfaltering belief which, had he been
more cultivated, might have thus expressed itself:

" If my bark sink, 't is to another sea "

THE LAND OF THE VIKINGS.

At the extremity of one of the branches of the Hardangerfjord is the little town of Odde.   This was the only place in
Norway where we had any difficulty in securing rooms.   As
the boat neared the wharf, I heard a dozen ladies whisper to
their husbands: " Now, dear, you stay and look after the

A STREET IN BERGEN.

luggage, and I 'll run on and get the rooms.''   Accordingly,
I used the same words to my friend, with the exception of the
endearing epithet.   I was afraid that might make him home-
sick.   Then I took my position near the gang-plank.

When we arrived, I was the first to step ashore, and I
started at a brisk walk toward the hotel.   Behind me I could
hear the rustling of many skirts, but, hardening my heart like
Pharaoh, I kept on.   At last, forgetting drapery and dignity,
the ladies passed me on the run.   This time I gallantly gave
way, and when, a moment later, I reached the hotel office,
I could have fancied myself on the floor of the Stock Exchange, since every lady there was fighting nobly for her
children and her absent lord.

" I want two beds," cried one.

" I wish for five beds," screamed another.

" Give me a room with blinds," exclaimed a third.

The female clerk, meantime, having completely lost her head, was calling off numbers like an auctioneer. Suddenly she turned to me, who had not yet opened my mouth, and almost paralyzed me with these words:

THE BERGEN FISH MARKET.

" Number 20 will do for you, *three beds and one cradle!* "

When I recovered from my swoon, I found that my friend had come up quietly after the battle, and had secured two single rooms.

Saying farewell to Odde, a day's delightful sail between majestic mountains brought us to one of Norway's most important cities — Bergen. Although we lingered here three days, we had the wonderful experience of continual sunshine. I rightly call it wonderful; for Bergen is the rainiest city in the world and is sarcastically called " The fatherland of drizzle." The people in Christiania claim that in Bergen when a horse sees a man *without* an umbrella, he shies! It is also said that a sea-captain, who was born in Bergen, and all his life had sailed between his native city and the outer world, came one day into its harbor when by chance the sun was shining. At once he put about and set forth to sea again, believing that

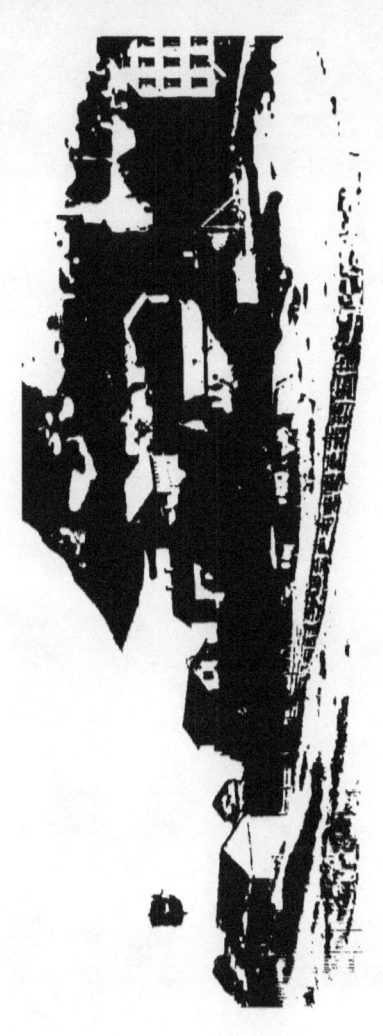

he had made a mistake in his port. As we approached the
pier at Bergen, I saw what, in the distance, appeared to be
a mob. It proved, however, to be the usual crowd which
gathers round the Bergen Fish Market.

This is not, after all, so strange if we reflect that fish is the
great commodity of Bergen, and that this city is the chief
distributing station for Norwegian fish to the entire world.
Several centuries ago, a company of German merchants, who
formed the famous Hanseatic League, established themselves
here and held for years within their hands the monopoly of
all the fishing trade of Norway, compelling even the Norwegian fishermen to send their catch of fish to Bergen for re-
shipment to other ports of Europe. It is true the league
exists no longer,
but its influence
still survives,
and nothing can
divert the trade
from following
in its ancient
channel. Over
the hills that rise
above the city
a splendid drive-
way has been
made. A Bergen
resident spoke of
it to me as "The
Drink Road."

MONSTERS OF THE DEEP.

"What is the meaning of so strange a title?" I inquired.

"It is so called," he said, "because it is constructed
wholly out of the profits derived from the sale of ardent
spirits." Observing my astonishment, he added: "Do you
not understand our famous liquor law in Bergen?"

BERGEN'S "DRINK ROAD."

I confessed my ignorance.

"Then let me explain it to you," he exclaimed. "Perhaps I can best do this," he added, "by pointing out to you that melancholy individual standing by the gang-plank. He used to be a liquor-seller here, but he has lost his 'spirits,' for our municipal government now has the sale of liquors entirely in its own hands. It first decides how many licenses are needed, and then, instead of giving them to private individuals, it grants them only to a responsible stock company. The books of this company must be at all times open to inspection, and all its rules are strictly under government control. Moreover, the company is not allowed to make more than five per cent. on its invested capital. All profits over that amount are given to public improvements, roads, parks, schools, or hospitals."

I asked if the law gave general satisfaction.

CURING FISH.

"We are delighted with it," was the answer. "It is now thirteen years since it was started, and all the prominent towns in Norway, except three, have followed our example. The liquors, in the first place, are all carefully selected. Secondly, the bars are not attractive gin-palaces, but plain rooms, with no seats for customers. No loitering on the premises is allowed. Only a small amount is sold at any one time. Children are not allowed to serve as messengers. Even the bar-tenders are appointed by the government, and wear a uniform and a number, by which they can be easily identified in case of complaint; and as a practical result," he added, "by taking the liquor traffic out of the hands of irresponsible

A BUSY DAY IN BERGEN.

agents the annual amount of ardent spirits sold has been reduced from twelve and a half to five and a half million quarts; and yet our Bergen company has earned each year a net profit of one hundred and twenty-five per cent, one hundred and twenty of which is, as I have said, applied to public charities!"

But to me the most interesting sight in Bergen was the grave of the Norwegian violinist, Ole Bull. His last appearance in America was in 1879 — too long ago perhaps for many

to recollect him — for, alas! even those who entertain the
public best are soon forgotten. But some of my readers
no doubt recall that Paganini of the North, tall and erect,
with large blue eyes and flaxen hair — the personification
of a valiant Norseman, whose fire and magnetism in this nineteenth century displayed themselves in music rather than in
maritime adventure.   As his old Viking ancestors had no doubt
wielded sword and battle-ax, so his bow was of such unusual

THE GRAVE OF OLE BULL.

length that no
one of inferior
strength and
stature could
have used it ad-
vantageously.

From this
musician's
grave one looks
off over the
lovely bay of
Bergen. This
peaceful view,
which he so
loved, produced
upon my mind,
in the soft

evening light, the same effect as did the music of that skillful
hand which now reposed beneath the flowers. To me his
playing was enchanting, and unlike that of any other violinist
I have ever heard. There was a quality in the tones that he
would call forth from his violin, which seemed as weird and
fascinating as the poetry of the sagas, and as mysterious as
the light which lingered on his mountains and fjords. What
wonder that his death in 1880 was deplored in Norway as a
national calamity?

Taking our leave reluctantly of
Bergen, we entered on what proved
to be one of the most delightful
features of our tour in Norway, a
sail of twenty-four hours along the
coast to the town of Molde. How
can I adequately describe that
most unique and memorable
journey? Our entire course lay
through a labyrinth of islands,
beyond which, every now and
then, we gained a glimpse of the
Atlantic rolling away toward the

OLE BULL.

horizon.   The proximity and number of these islands astonished me.   For, hour after hour, they would come into
sight, wheel by us slowly, and then disappear, to be succeeded
by their counterparts.   We went down to dinner or to our
staterooms, yet when we came on deck again, islands
still surrounded us.   We saw them glittering in the sunset
ere we went to sleep, and in the morning we were once more
environed by them.   Sometimes I could have fancied that
they were sailing with us, like a vast convoy of protecting
gunboats, moving when we moved, halting when we halted,
patient and motionless till we resumed our voyage.

Meantime, just opposite these islands, is the coast,— a
grand succession of bold headlands and dark, gloomy mountains, beyond which always are still higher summits capped

with snow. At frequent intervals some beautiful fjord leads inward, like the entrance to a citadel; and here and there, within a sheltered nook, we see some fishing hamlet crouching on the sand. This is surely the perfection of ocean travel. For, though this mountain-bordered channel is hundreds of miles in length, the sea within it is as smooth as a canal. Once only throughout the day was the great swell

A WONDERFUL PANORAMA.

of the Atlantic felt, when for a little space the island breakwater was gone.

Our sail along the coast had, late at night, a most appropriate ending in our arrival at Molde. There are few places in the world more beautiful. It lies upon the bank of a fjord, on the opposite side of which is an array of snowy mountains forty miles in length. Molde is sometimes called the "Interlaken of Norway," but that does not by any means describe it. For here there is no single mountain, like the Jungfrau, to compel our homage, but rather a long series of majestic peaks, resembling a line of icebergs drifting in crystal splendor from the polar sea.

Filled with enthusiasm over this splendid spectacle, we left the steamer, and soon found ourselves within a comfortable hotel. It was the hour of midnight, but, far from being dark, the eastern sky was even then brightening with the coming dawn. A party of excursionists was just returning from a mountain climb. Some passengers were embarking on the steamer we had left. Supper or breakfast (I know not which to call it) was awaiting us. Under such circumstances it seemed ridiculous to go to bed. Accordingly, we laughed and chatted on the balcony, until a wretched man thrust out his head from an adjoining window, and remarked:

" My friends, I am glad to see you happy, but I have just returned from the North Cape. I have n't slept for eight nights. It seems quite dark here by comparison, and I was hopeful of a good night's rest. Would you just as lief postpone your fun until you get inside the Arctic circle?"

This pathetic appeal could not be resisted, and asking his forgiveness, we retired.

Taking leave of Molde one pleasant afternoon, we sailed across its beautiful fjord to explore the snow-capped mountains opposite. It was upon this voyage that I was taught the bitter lesson never to trust my baggage to a Norwegian, merely because he claims to be able to speak English. Upon the deck of our little steamer stood that day a man, upon whose hatband I read the legend that he was the proprietor of a hotel at Veblungsnäs, where we proposed to spend the night. Approaching him, therefore, I inquired:

" Can you speak English?"

He smiled upon me sweetly, and replied, " O, yes."

Innocent of the awful fact that this was the whole extent of his vocabulary, I continued:

" When we arrive, will you bring my valise ashore, while I go at once to the hotel to secure rooms?"

" O, yes."

Ten minutes later we reached our landing pier. I left the

boat, as I had said, and hurried on to the hotel. I presently beheld the old proprietor coming from the wharf, but without my satchel.

VIEW FROM MOLDE.

" What does this mean?" I cried; " did you not bring my valise off the steamer?"

" O, yes."

"Where is it, then? Is it not on there still?"

" O, yes."

"Mercy on me! Is not that the steamer going off with my valise on board?"

"O, yes!"

"Well, are you not a monumental idiot, then?"

"O, yes!"

It took me three days to recover that valise; and the important lesson of " *O, yes,*" was effectually learned.

Early next morning we took leave of Veblungsnäs, and drove directly towards the Romsdal, one of the finest valleys in all Norway. Before us, like a mighty sentinel, the imposing Romsdalhorn rose, dark with somber shadows, to an altitude of five thousand and ninety feet. The peak itself, five hundred feet in height, is said to be almost as dangerous to ascend as the appalling Matterhorn, not only on account of its perpendicular sides, but also from the crumbling nature of the rock, which renders it impossible to fasten iron bars in its surface.

Some years ago, an English tourist, after a number of unsuccessful efforts, finally reached the summit of this moun-

tain. He was, of course, exultant. The inhabitants of the
valley had told him that the conquest of the Romsdalhorn
was hopeless, and no tradition existed among them that its
ascent had ever been made. Nevertheless, when the success-
ful climber finally stood upon the mountain's crest, he found
to his astonishment and regret that he was not the first
man who had gained this victory. A mound of stones,
heaped up there as a monument, proved beyond doubt that
at some unknown epoch some one had been there before him.

Driving around the base of this majestic mountain, we
found ourselves within a narrow gorge shut in by savage
cliffs, with barely space enough between them for the carriage-
road and a wild torrent rushing toward the sea. One wall of
this ravine is singu-   larly weird and
awe - inspir-   ing. A multitude of   crags and

pinnacles, splintered and shattered by the lightning's bolts, stand out in sharp relief against the sky, as if some monsters, hidden on the other side, were raising o'er the brink of these stupendous precipices their outstretched hands and tapering fingers in warning or in supplication. These strange, fantastic forms are in the evening light so ghostly and uncanny, that they appear to the Norwegian peasants like demons dancing glee-

fully upon the mountain tops. Hence the pinnacles are called the "Witches' Peaks."

It was while riding through this gorge that I heard a tourist complaining that Norway had no ruins. In one sense this is true, for, owing to the fact

THE WITCHES' PEAKS.

that the feudal system never existed here, castles and strong-holds are nowhere to be found. But Norway surely can dispense with any crumbling works of man. Amidst the ruins of her everlasting mountains and stupendous fjords, grooved by the glaciers when the earth was young, all remnants of man's handiwork would seem like ant-hills made but an hour ago.

Toward evening, at the head of the Romsdal Valley, we reached the station of Stuflaaten, where we were to sleep. Our spirits sank as we approached it. Nothing, apparently, could be less inviting. But here, as in so many other instances, we found the accommodations excellent. It is true, the beds possessed the usual Norwegian fault—an insufficient length. Tall travelers, who object to having their limbs closed under them at

STUFLAATEN.

night, like the blades of a jack-knife, frequently sleep on the floor in Norway.

" I cannot lie in one of these beds," exclaimed my friend; which, for a lawyer, seemed to me a remarkable admission!

Never shall I forget the dining-room at Stuflaaten. Here we were first attracted by the fireplace. It was a chimney built out from the corner, with space behind for a warm cupboard. The opening for fuel was so narrow that sticks were placed upright upon the hearth. Beside this were two rocking-chairs (almost unheard of luxuries in any part of Europe), and sinking into these, we thought

A NEW ENGLAND SOUVENIR.

of home. The influence of that American article of furniture was, I fear, depressing, for soon my friend remarked:

"How far we are from dear New England! If I could only see one object here which really came from there, how happy I should be!"

"Look at that clock upon the wall," I responded; "that has a familiar look. Perhaps that came from 'dear New England!'"

"Nonsense," he answered; "how could anything made in New England find its way here almost within the Arctic circle?"

TRONDHJEM.

"Well," I exclaimed, "where is the land that Yankee inventions have not entered? Let us put it to the test." Accordingly, stepping to the clock, I opened it and read these words: "Made by Jerome & Co., New Haven, Conn."

Returning once more through the Romsdal, Veblungsnäs, and Molde, we sailed again, for twelve hours, along the Norway coast to reach the city of Trondhjem. Although less beautifully situated than Bergen, Molde, or Christiania, in point of historic interest, Trondhjem is superior to them all. For here lived the old Norwegian kings, and the town can boast of a continuous existence for a thousand years. It also enjoys the proud distinction of having the most northern railway station in the world, for from this city, which is in the latitude of Iceland, a railroad now extends three hundred and fifty miles southward to Christiania.

A NORWEGIAN RAILWAY.

Upon this road are run some cars which are facetiously called "sleepers"; but they are such as Mr. George M. Pullman would see only in an acute attack of nightmare. The road being a narrow-gauge one, the car is not much wider than an omnibus. The berth (if the name can be applied to such a coffin-like contrivance) is formed by pulling narrow cushion-seats together. On these is placed one pillow, but no blanket and no mattress,—simply a pillow,—nothing more! From the feeling, I should say that my pillow consisted of a small boulder covered with cotton. But what, think you, is the upper berth? It is a hammock, swung on hooks, and sagging down to within a foot of the lower couch. Now, it requires some skill to get into a hammock anywhere; but to climb into one that is hung four feet above the floor of a moving railroad car, calls for the

A RAILWAY STATION.

agility of an acrobat. After my experience that night, I feel perfectly qualified to perform on the trapeze, for since I weighed but one hundred and forty pounds, while my friend tipped the

A NORWEGIAN HARBOR.

scales at two hundred and fifty, I thought it was safer for me to occupy the upper story. Another difficulty met with in that memorable journey was to keep covered up. There was no heat in the car. At every respiration, we could see our breath. This was, however, a consolation, since it assured us that we were still alive. Wraps of all kinds were needed, but the space was limited. There was, for example, in my hammock, room for myself alone; or without me, for my traveling-rug, overcoat, and pillow. But when we were all in together, the hammock was continually overflowing. Accordingly, every fifteen minutes during that awful night, my friend would start up in abject terror, dreaming that he was being buried beneath a Norway avalanche.

I never think of Trondhjem without recalling, also, an experience in a Norwegian barber-shop. I knew that it was tempting Providence to enter it, for shaving in Norway is still a kind of surgical operation. But for some time a coldness had existed between my razors and myself. The edge of our friendship had become dulled. Accordingly, I made the venture. Before me, as I entered, stood a man with a head of hair like Rubenstein's, and a mouth like a miniature fjord.

TOURING ON FOOT.

" Do you speak English? " I began.

" Nay."

" Sprechen sie Deutsch? "

" Nay."

" Parlez-vous Français? "

" Nay."

" Parlate Italiano? "

" Nay."

" Well, one thing is sure, then," I said; " you will not talk me to death, anyway! "

Having made the most graceful gestures of which I was capable to indicate what I wanted, I settled myself in a hard chair and laid my head against a rest resembling the vise furnished by a photographer when he asks you " to look pleasant." The preliminaries being over, the Norwegian Figaro took his razor and made one awful never-to-be-forgotten swoop at my cheek as if he were mowing grain with a scythe! I gave a roar like a Norwegian waterfall and bounded from the chair in agony! When I had fully wiped away my blood and tears, I asked him faintly:

A VILLAGE MAIDEN.

" Have you any ether? "

" Nay."

" Any laughing-gas? "

" Nay."

" Any cocaine? "

" Nay."

" Well, then," I exclaimed, " will you please go over there and ' nay ' by yourself while I finish this operation with my own hands? "

He seemed to understand me, and retreated to a corner. When all was over, he pointed to a bowl at which I saw my friend gazing with that peculiarly sad expression which he invariably assumed when thinking of his family. I soon discovered the cause, for from the centre of this wash-bowl rose a little fountain about a foot in height, which seemed to him a facsimile of the one on Boston Common. I compre-

ENTRANCE TO A FJORD.

hended that I was to wash in this fountain; but how to do it was a mystery. At last I cautiously thrust one side of my face into it, and instantly the water shot up over my ear and fell upon the other side. I turned my face, and the ascending current carromed on my nose, ran down my neck, and made a change of toilet absolutely necessary. When, therefore, my friend had called a cab to take me home, I asked the barber what I should pay him. By gestures he expressed to me the sum equivalent to three cents.

"What," I exclaimed, "nothing extra for the court-plaster?"

"Nay."

"And nothing for the privilege of shaving myself?"

"Nay."

"And you don't charge for the fountain, either?"

" Nay.'

"Well," I exclaimed as I rode away, " I can truly say that never before have I received so much for my money."

This city of the north has one extremely interesting building—its cathedral. As a rule, Scandinavian churches are not worth a visit; but this is a notable exception. More than three hundred years before Columbus landed on San Salvador this building held a proud position. Its finest carving dates from the eleventh century. At one time pilgrims came here from all northern Europe, and laid their gold and jewels on its shrines. But at the period of the Reformation all this was changed. Iconoclasts defaced its carving, cast down its statues, sacked the church, and packed its treasures in a ship, which, as if cursed by an offended Deity, foundered at sea.

On entering the ancient edifice, we were delighted with its delicate stone-tracing. The material is a bluish slate, which gives to the whole church a softness and a beauty difficult to

TRONDHJEM CATHEDRAL.

equal, and blends most admirably with its columns of white marble. A part of the cathedral was, however, closed to us, for all the ruin once wrought here is being carefully effaced by systematic restoration. The government contributes for

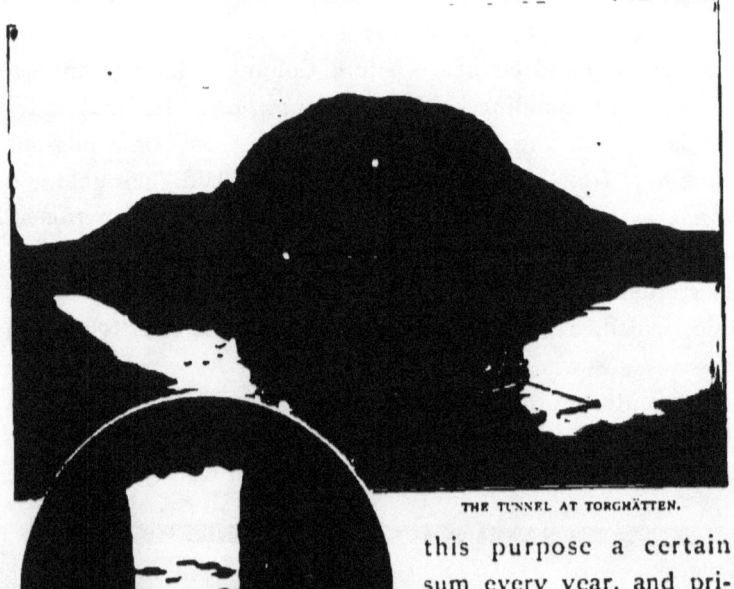

THE TUNNEL AT TORGHÄTTEN.

this purpose a certain sum every year, and private individuals help on the work from genuine love of art, as well as from patriotic motives. The old designs are being followed, and hence, in time, this old cathedral will in every feature come to be a reproduction of the original structure.

A few days after reaching Trondhjem, we found ourselves embarking for another ocean journey. This time our destination was the northern limit of the continent. For a Norwegian tour naturally divides itself into three parts. The first consists of driving through the mountainous interior; the

second is the ex-
ploration of its
noble fjords;
the third is the
voyage from
Trondhjem to
the North Cape.
This voyage,
in fast excursion
steamers, is now

AN EXCURSION STEAMER.

made in about four days, an equal number being occupied in
returning. "Eight days?" the reader will perhaps exclaim;
"why, that is longer than a voyage across the Atlantic." In
actual duration, yes; but otherwise the two excursions are
entirely different. For almost all the way you follow so
closely the fringe of islands that there is little danger of
rough weather, while the mainland is constantly in sight.

Some twenty-four hours after leaving Trondhjem, our
steamer halted at an island, up whose precipitous side we
climbed five hundred feet to view a natural tunnel perfo-
rating an entire mountain. Through this we gained a charming telescopic vista of the ocean and its island belt. The tunnel is six hundred feet in length, and in some places two hundred feet in height. So smooth and perpendicular are its
walls, that it appears almost incredible that human agency

ONE OF THE LOFFODENS.

has not assisted
in this strange
formation. But
scientists say
that it was
accomplished
entirely by the
waves, when all
this rock-bound

coast was covered by the sea. Leaving this curious freak of
nature, another memorable feature of our northern voyage
soon greeted us,—the Loffoden Islands. These form a
broken chain one hundred and thirty miles in length. The
scenery in their vicinity is perhaps the finest on the Norway
coast, and as we watched it with delight, the captain told us
of his voyages here in winter, and I now learned, to my astonishment that freight-steamers make their regular trips, all

FISHING ON THE COAST.

winter long, round the North Cape to Vadso, on the Arctic
coast. They encounter fearful storms at times, but rarely any
icebergs. We have, it seems, a monopoly of these floating
monsters on our side of the Atlantic, borne west and south
by the current off the coast of Greenland.

Of course, these wintry voyages are performed in darkness, for Night then reigns here with as much supremacy as
Day in summer. The lights on the steamers are, therefore,
kept constantly burning. Yet, strange to say, this is the
period of greatest activity among these islands. Winter is the
Norwegian fisherman's harvest-time. The only light neces-

SCENE FROM BROTHANSDALEN.

sary to carry on the work is that of the Aurora Borealis and the brilliant stars. From twenty to twenty-five millions of cod are captured here each winter, and twenty-five thousand people are employed in the trade.

TROMSÖ.

Soon after leaving the Loffodens we arrived at Tromsö, the city of the Lapps. It had the appearance of a pretty village as we viewed it from a distance; but soon the sense of sight was wholly lost in the prominence given to another of our senses. The carcass of a whale was floating in the harbor. It had been speared and towed in hither to be

LAPLANDERS.

cut in pieces. The blubber was being boiled in kettles on the shore. The impression which this made on my olfactory nerves is something for which language is inadequate. The odor was as colossal as the fish itself. I never sympathized sufficiently with Jonah till I went to Tromsö!

Soon after landing here, a walk of an hour brought us to a settlement of Lapps, consisting of some very primitive tents. My first impression of these people was, and still is, that any one of them could have effectually concealed

REINDEER
AND SLEDGE.

his identity by
taking a bath.
They all have
dirty, wizened faces, high cheekbones, flat noses, and mouths
that yawn like caverns. Their beards are so peculiarly tufted
that they look like worn-out Astrachan fur. I could almost
suppose that in rigorous winters the reindeer, while their masters slept, had nibbled at their cheeks. The men are about
five feet high, the women four;
but they are tough and hardy,
like most dwarfs. Dickens
could have found among them
countless models for his hid-
eous Quilp.

A LITTLE LAPP.

Advancing to one of their
huts, we peered into the interior. Upon the ground was
smoldering a small fire, part
of the smoke from which escaped through an opening in
the roof. The inmates scarcely
noticed us, until my artist pro-

duced his camera. Then there was instantly a general stampede.
One woman seized her baby and rushed forth, as if a demon
had molested her. The cause of this confusion, however, was
not fear, nor even modesty, but avarice, pure and simple.
They understood perfectly what the camera was, and wanted
a good price for being photographed. Three shillings was

LIFE IN LAPLAND.

at first demanded for a picture, but finally we compromised
by giving half that sum.

Among these Laplanders, the clothing of both men and
women is made of reindeer skin, worn with the hardened pelt
outside. These garments last indefinitely, and are sometimes
bequeathed from one generation to another. The Lapp com-
plexion looks like leather. Even the babies have a shriveled
look, resembling that of monkeys. This is not strange, however, for both men and women are great consumers of
tobacco. Their huts are always full of smoke, till finally the
inmates become smoke-dried within and without. This, in
turn, produces thirst. Hence we were not surprised to learn
that they are inordinately fond of ardent spirits. In fact,

when a Norwegian wishes to remonstrate with a friend who is inclined to drink to excess, he will often say to him, "Don't make a Lapp of yourself!"

Bidding farewell to Tromsö and the Laplanders, the next day brought us to the most northern town in the world — Hammerfest. It was a great surprise to me to see, in such proximity to the North Pole, a town of about three thousand inhabitants, with schools, a church, a telegraph station, and a weekly newspaper! The snow-streaked mountains in the distance gave me the only hint of winter that I had; and I could hardly realize that I was here two hundred miles farther north than Bering's Strait, and in about the same latitude in which, on our side of the Atlantic, the gallant Sir John Franklin perished in the ice. The cause of this, however, is not difficult to trace.

The influence of the Gulf Stream is felt powerfully even here. For here it is that the great ocean current practically dies, bequeathing to these fishermen of Hammerfest, for

HAMMERFEST.

their firewood, the treasures it has so long carried on its bosom, such as the trunks of palm-trees, and the vegetation of the

THE GULF STREAM'S TERMINUS.

tropics. It is an extraordinary fact that while the harbor of Christiania, one thousand miles farther south, is frozen over three months every winter, this bay of Hammerfest, only sixty miles from the North Cape, is never closed on account of ice.

An interesting object in Hammerfest is the meridian shaft, which marks the number of degrees between this town and the mouth of the Danube, on the Black Sea. The mention made upon this column of that other terminus of measurement, so far distant in the South of Europe, reminded us by contrast of one more advantage which this high latitude possesses — the greater rapidity of its vegetation. When the sun once appears within this polar region, it comes to stay. Nature immediately makes amends for her long seclusion. For three months the sunshine is well-nigh incessant. There is no

THE MERIDIAN SHAFT.

loss of time at night. The flowers do not close in sleep. All vegetation rushes to maturity. Thus vegetables in the Arctic circle will sometimes grow three inches in a single day, and although planted six weeks later than those in Christiania, they are ready for the table at the same time.

Sailing finally from Hammerfest, a voyage of seven hours brought us to our destination — the North Cape. I looked upon it with that passionate eager-ness born of long years of anticipa-tion, and felt at once a thrill of satisfaction, in the absence of all disappoint-ment. For my ideal of that famous promon-tory could not be more perfect-ly realized than in this dark-browed, majestic

NORWEGIAN FLORA.

headland, rising with perpendicular cliffs, one thousand feet in height, from the still darker ocean at its base. It is, in reality, an island, divided from the mainland by a narrow strait, like a gigantic sentinel stationed in advance to guard the coast of Europe from the Arctic storms.

Embarking here in boats, we drew still nearer to this monstrous cliff. From this point it resembles a stupendous fortress surmounted by an esplanade. For in that prehis-toric age, when northern Europe was enveloped in an icy mantle, huge glaciers in their southward march planed down its summit to a level surface. The climbing of the cliff, though safe, is quite exhausting. Ropes are, however, hung

HARBOR OF HAMMERFEST.

at different points, and, holding on to these, we slowly crept
up to its southern parapet.   Thence a laborious walk of fifteen minutes brought us at last to the highest elevation,
marked by a granite monument erected to commemorate
King Oscar's visit to the place in 1873.

It is a wonderfully impressive moment when one stands
thus on the northern boundary of Europe, so near and yet so
far from the North Pole.   It seemed to me as if the outer-
most limit of our planet had been reached.   Nowhere, not
even in the desert, have I felt so utterly remote from civilization, or so near to the infinitude of space.

But presently from our steamer, anchored near the base,
some rockets rose and burst in fiery showers far below us.   It
was a signal for us to be on our guard.   I looked at my
watch.   It was exactly five minutes before midnight.   Advancing, therefore, to the edge of the cliff, I looked upon a unique
and never-to-be-forgotten scene.   Below, beyond me, and on
either side, lay   in sublime and awful solitude   the Arctic sea,
stretch-   ing away

NORTH CAPE.

STUPENDOUS CLIFFS.

to that still un-
discovered re-
gion of the
north, which,
with its fatal
charm, has lured
so many brave
explorers to
their doom.

Straight from
the polar sea,
apparently, the
wondrous north-
ern light (an
opalescent radi-
ance born of the twilight and the dawn) came stealing o'er
the waters like a benediction; and to enhance its mystery
and beauty, when I looked northward over the rounded

shoulder of the
globe, I saw the
MIDNIGHT SUN.

At this great
height and
northern lati-
tude it did not
sink to the hori-
zon, but merely
paused, appar-
ently some twen-
ty feet above the
waves, then
gradually rose
again. It was
the last of count-

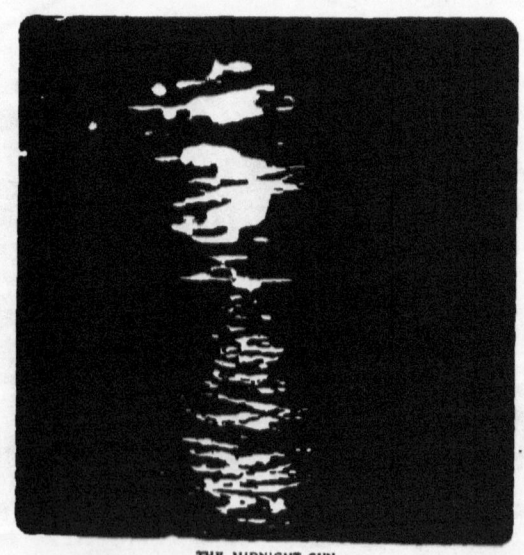

THE MIDNIGHT SUN.

less sunsets which had that day been following each other
round the globe.   It was the first of countless sunrises which,
hour after hour, in so many continents would wake to life
again a sleeping world.   I have seen many impressive sights
in many lands, but nothing, until Time for me shall be no
more, can equal in solemnity the hour when, standing on this
threshold of a continent, and on the edge of this immeasur-
able sea, I watched, without one moment's interval of darkness, the Past transform itself into the Present, and Yesterday
become To-day.

KING OSCAR'S MONUMENT — NORTH CAPE.

SWITZERLAND

SWITZERLAND

THE Parsees say that mountains are the heads of the long pins that bind the world together. Geologists assure us that they are merely wrinkles on the face of Mother Earth, while we all know that, relatively to the world's diameter, the highest elevation of our planet is but the thickness of a hair laid on an ordinary globe.

But these comparisons do not affect the grandeur of the peaks themselves, when we behold them face to face, crowned with unmeasured miles of snow, girded with glaciers as with coats of mail, and towering up among the clouds as though to storm the very heights of Heaven. If it be true, as some have claimed, that travel blunts the edge of enjoyment, and renders one indifferent and *blasé*, it is true only of those arti-

A CHATEAU NEAR INTERLAKEN.

ficial charms which form the attraction of great cities and the pleasure-haunts of men. These may at last grow wearisome. But Nature wears a freshness and a glory that can never fade.

INTERLAKEN.

Continual worship at her shrine increases our desire for that happiness which only Nature gives, and adds to our capacity for its appreciation.

Switzerland, then, of all countries in the world, is the one of which the traveler is likely to tire least. The vision of its kingly Alps must always thrill the heart with exultation. Its noble roads and unsurpassed hotels make rest or travel on its heights delightful; while the keen tonic of its mountain air restores the jaded frame, as ancients dreamed a draught would do from the pure fountain of perpetual youth.

One of the most attractive gateways to this land of mountains is Interlaken. All tourists in Switzerland come hither, almost of necessity. No other point is quite so central for excursions. None is more easy of approach. As its name

indicates, it lies between two famous lakes which rival one
another in respect to beauty.   Before it, also, are the charming vales of Lauterbrunnen and Grindelwald, which lead one
into the very heart of the Bernese Oberland.   Moreover, from
sixty to eighty thousand people come here every year to
render homage to the peerless sovereign who holds court at
Interlaken.   There is no need to name the peak to which I
thus allude, for everywhere in Interlaken we discern the crowning glory of the place — beside which all others fade —
the lovely Jungfrau, queen of Alpine heights.   Her grand,
resplendent form fills the entire space between the encircling
peaks, and forms a dazzling center-piece of ice and snow,
nearly fourteen thousand feet in height.   It is a never-ending
pleasure to rest upon the broad piazzas of Interlaken's palatial hotels, and gaze upon this radiant mount.   It sometimes
looks like a great white cloud forever anchored in one place, but
oftener sparkles as if covered with a robe of diamonds; mantled,
as it is, with snows of virgin purity from base to heaven-pierc-
ing summit.

JUNGFRAU FROM INTERLAKEN.

Yet were we to examine closely a single section of the Jungfrau, we should discover that its shoulders are covered with enormous snow-fields, the origin of stupendous avalanches. For amid all this beauty there is much here that

PARLIAMENT BUILDINGS, BERNE.

is harsh and terrible. Appalling precipices, dangerous crevasses, and well-nigh constant falls of hundreds of tons of rock and ice, render the wooing of this "Maiden of the Alps" a difficult undertaking. In fact, the name Jungfrau, or Maiden, was given to the mountain, because its pure summit seemed destined to remain forever virgin to the tread of man. Many had sought to make her conquest, but in vain. At last, however, in 1811 (nearly thirty years after the subjugation of Mont Blanc), two brothers gained the .crest; and since that time its icy slopes have reflected the forms of many ambitious and courageous travelers.

No tourist who has been at Interlaken on a pleasant evening can possibly forget the vision which presents itself as day reluctantly retires from the Jungfrau at the approach of night.

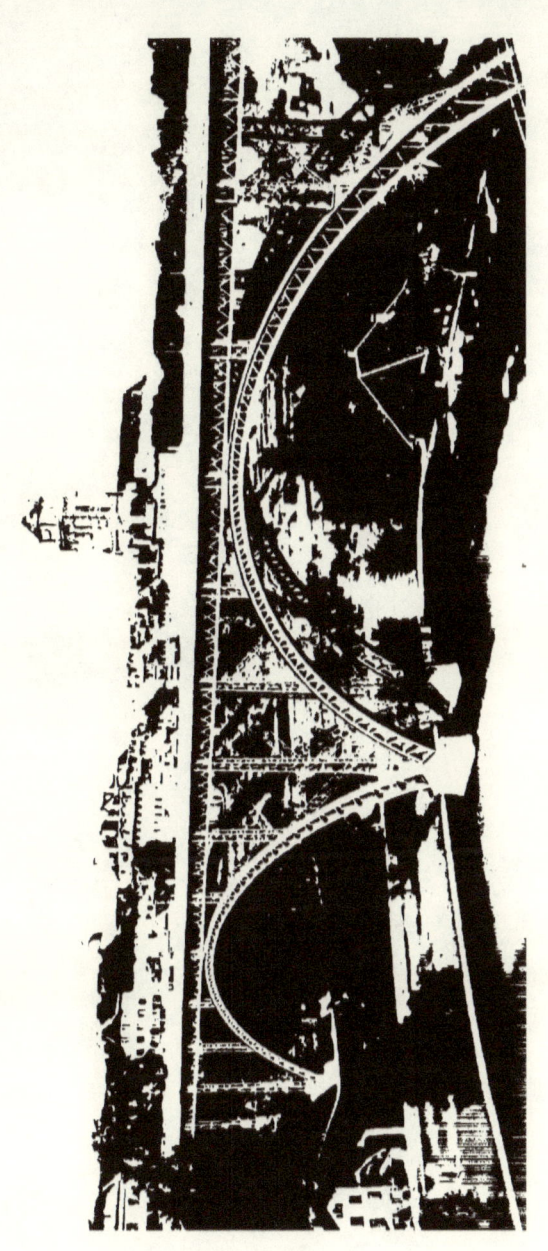

SWITZERLAND

SUNSET AT INTERLAKEN.

The sun is low;
Yon peak of snow
Is purpling 'neath the sunset glow;
The rosy light
Makes richly bright
The Jungfrau's veil of snowy white.

From vales that sleep
Night's shadows creep
To take possession of the steep;
While, as they rise,
The western skies
Seem loth to leave so fair a prize.

The light of Day
Still loves to stay
And round that pearly summit play;
How fair a sight,
That plain of light
Contended for by Day and Night!

SWITZERLAND

Now fainter shines.
As Day declines,
The lustrous height which he resigns;
The shadows gain
Th' illumined plain;
The Jungfrau pales, as if in pain.

ON LAKE THUN.

When daylight dies,
The azure skies
Seem sparkling with a thousand eyes,
Which watch with grace
From depths of space
The sleeping Jungfrau's lovely face.

And when is born
The ruddy Dawn,
Forerunner of the coming Morn,
Along the skies
It quickly flies
To kiss the Maiden's opening eyes.

The timid flush,
The rosy blush,
Which then o'er brow and face do rush,
Are pure and fair
Beyond compare,
Resplendent in the illumined air.

And thus alway,
By night or day,
Her varying suitors homage pay;
And tinged with rose,
Or white with snows,
The same fair radiant form she shows.

I have said that Interlaken was an admirable place from
which to make excursions.   Shall we not put this to the proof
by entering now the charming and romantic vale of Lauterbrunnen, dainty and lovely as a dimple in the cheek of Nature?
It is only half a mile in width, and is bounded on both sides by
lofty mountains, over which the winter's sun can hardly climb
till midday.   And yet luxuriant vegetation covers it, as with
an emerald carpet.   The bases of these mountains seem to rest
on flowers.   The awful scenery which surrounds it makes it seem
doubly sweet and fair; and one can hardly imagine a more
striking picture than that of this
peaceful valley, looking smilingly
up into the stern and savage faces
of the monsters which environ it,
as if unconscious of its helplessness, or trusting confidently in
their mercy.

A little distance
up the valley, we
note its most re-
markable feature,
the Fall of the
Staubbach, or
"Dust-brook,"
which here leaps
boldly over the
brow of the
mountain,

THE STAUBBACH.

VALLEY OF LAUTERBRUNNEN.

nine hundred and eighty feet above us. Long before it reaches the ground, it is converted into a vast, diaphanous cloud of spray, which the breeze scatters into thousands of fantastic wreaths. Whenever the sunlight streams directly through this, the effect is marvelous. It then resembles a transparent veil of silvery lace, woven with all the colors of the rainbow, fluttering from the fir-clad rocks. Byron compared it to the tail of a white horse, streaming in the wind; but Goethe's description is best, when he exclaims:

" In clouds of spray,
Like silver dust,
It veils the rock
In rainbow hues;
And dancing down
With music soft,
Is lost in air."

But the ambitious traveler will ascend far higher than the summit of this waterfall to stand upon the mighty cliffs which line the valley like gigantic walls.

GOING TO MÜRREN.

ZÜRICH.

COMFORT IN SWITZERLAND.

The task is easily accomplished now. Ten years ago it was an arduous climb, on horseback or on foot; but now an electric railroad winds for miles along the edge of frightful precipices, and (where a vertical ascent is absolutely necessary) another kind of car lifts one a thousand feet or so toward heaven, as smoothly and as swiftly as a hotel elevator.

Truly the visitor of a dozen years ago perceives amazing changes to-day among the Alps. Where, formerly, a man would hardly dare to go on foot, trains now ascend with myriads of travelers! Hotels and even railroad stations up among the clouds have driven from the lofty crags the eagle and the chamois. This to the genuine Alpine climber seems like sacrilege; but, after all, what contributors to the happiness of mankind these mountain railroads are! Without them, few would venture here; and all the pageantry of Nature in these upper regions

MODERN ALPINE CLIMBING.

would unfold itself through the revolving years with scarce an eye to note its beauty or voice to tell its glories to the world.

In startling contrast to my first ascent to the place, now many years ago,

MÜRREN.

it was by this luxurious mode of travel that I recently approached the little village known as Mürren. It is the loftiest hamlet in all Switzerland, consisting of a cluster of Swiss cottages, whose roofs, heavily freighted with protecting stones, project beyond the walls like broad-brimmed hats. So singular is the appearance of a village at this dizzy height, that one is tempted to believe that the houses had been blown up from the valley by some reckless blast, and dropped at random on the lonely tableland.

Yet here, to our astonishment, we find hotels, which somehow year by year outlive the horrors of the Alpine winter, and in the summer season welcome their hundreds of adventurous guests. But, after all, where in Switzerland is there not a hotel? Fast as the arteries of travel are extended, on every prominent point commanding a fine view is planted a hotel, a forerunner of the world of travel. This is, in fact, one of the charms of Switzerland. The Andes and Himalayas may possess higher peaks and grander glaciers; but there one cannot (as among the Alps) ride all day long on perfect roads, and in the evening sit down to a well-cooked dinner, hear music on a broad veranda, consult the latest newspapers, and sleep in a comfortable bed.

Even before the advent of the railroad, I was a thousand-fold repaid for climbing up to Mürren; for here so closely do the Alpine Titans press on every side, that if Mohammed had ever found his way hither, he might well have believed that the mountains were coming to him, and not he to the mountains.

The surrounding summits reveal to the astonished sight heights, lengths, and depths which overwhelm one with sublimity. What seemed an hour ago mere glistening mounds are now transformed by the grandeur of this Olympian eleva-tion into vast snowfields, miles in length, or into seas of ice, which pour down through the valleys in slow-moving floods. In early summer, too, one hears at frequent inter-vals the roar of some tremen-dous avalanche on the great mountains oppo-

A HOTEL AT MÜRREN.

site, from which the tourist is separated only by a yawning gulf.

Never shall I forget the morning when I stood here wait-ing for the sunrise view. There was none of that crowd of jab-

bering tourists who often profane the summit of the Rigi, and
seem to measure the extent of their pleasure by the noise they
make. I was well-nigh alone. When I emerged from the
hotel, a purple line was visible in the east, but clouds and
mists half veiled the mountains from my sight. At length,
however, noiselessly but steadily, a hidden hand seemed
to draw back the misty curtain of the night. Slowly the
giant forms molded themselves from darkness into light,
until their foreheads first, and then each fold and outline
of their dazzling shapes, stood forth in bold relief against the
sky. The glaciers sparkled with the first bright beams like
jeweled highways of the gods, — till, finally, as the sun's
disk came fairly into view, the whole vast range glowed like a
wall of tinted porcelain. It seemed as if a thousand sacred
fires had been kindled on these mountain altars, in glad
response to the triumphant greeting of the god of day.

On descending from Mürren, the tourist is attracted to
another famous object, only a few miles from Interlaken, —
the glacier of Grindelwald.

A VIEW FROM MÜRREN.

MÜRREN—HOTEL DES ALPES.

It was while visiting this sea of ice that my guide suddenly turned and asked me with a smile, "Are you a clergyman?"

I answered that I could not claim that flattering distinction, but begged to know the reason of his question. "Because," he said, "clergymen seem to be unlucky in Grindelwald; all the accidents that take place here somehow happen to them."

As we were at that moment just about to venture on the ice, I naturally recalled Charles Lamb's reply when he was requested to say grace at dinner. "What," he

A GLACIER.

exclaimed, "are there no clergymen present? Then I will say, the Lord be thanked!"

A moment or two later we entered the well-known cavern in this glacier — a strange and chilling passageway, two hundred feet in length, cut in the solid ice, whose gleaming walls and roof seemed to be made of polished silver.

As I was picking my way safely, though shiveringly, through this huge refrigerator, I asked my guide to tell me about one of the clerical misfortunes which had made him suspicious of gentlemen of the cloth. He turned and looked at me curiously. "You know, of course, the fate of our pastor, M. Mouron?" he exclaimed. I confessed my ignorance.

A CHILLING PASSAGEWAY.

"Then come with me," he said. Accordingly, emerging from the cavern, we climbed for nearly an hour over great blocks of ice, until we came to a profound abyss. Suspended from the frozen parapet a mass of icicles pointed mysteriously down like ghostly fingers. Then all was dark. "It was by falling down this," said the guide, "that the pastor of Grindelwald lost his life. He was seeking one day to ascertain its depth by casting stones into its cavernous maw and counting till he heard the sound of their arrival at the bottom of the abyss. Once, in his eagerness, he placed his staff against the opposite edge, leaned over and listened. Suddenly the ice gave way, and he fell headlong into the crevasse. His guide ran breathless to the village and

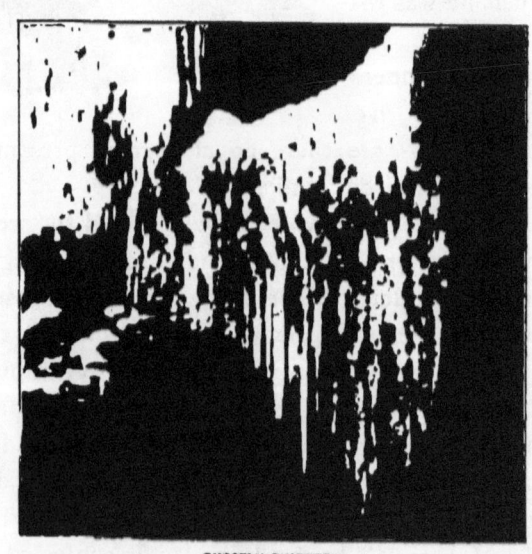

GHOSTLY FINGERS.

informed the people of their loss.   But, to his horror, he
found that he himself was looked upon with suspicion.   In
fact, some went so far as to say that he must have murdered
their pastor, and robbed him of his watch and purse.

"The guides of Grindelwald, however, who felt themselves insulted at this accusation, united and agreed that one
of their number (chosen by lot) should, at the peril of his life,
descend into this crevasse to establish the innocence of the

LAUSANNE.

accused.   The lot was drawn by
one of the bravest of them all, a
man named Bergenen.   The whole
village assembled on the flood of
ice to witness the result of the search.   After partaking of
the sacrament, Bergenen fastened a rope around his waist
and a lantern to his neck.   In one hand he took a bell.
In the other he grasped his iron-pointed staff to keep himself from the sharp edges.   Four men then carefully lowered
him down.   Twice, on the point of suffocation, he rang the

HAY-MAKING.

bell and was drawn up. Finally a heavier weight was felt upon the rope, and Bergenen reappeared, bringing the body of the pastor from a depth of seven hundred and fifty feet. A mighty shout went up from the guides and populace as well. The man was innocent. Both watch and purse were found upon the corpse!"

As we returned from Grindelwald to Interlaken, we often paused to note the peasants toiling in the fields. So far as their appearance was concerned, we might have supposed them laborers on a Vermont farm; but their low carts were quite unlike

UPON THE HEIGHTS.

our country hayracks; and the appearance of a single ox, harnessed with ropes around his horns, presented an amusing contrast to the sturdy beasts which, bound together by the yoke, drag to our barns their loads of fragrant hay. Women, of course, were working with the men; but female laborers in Switzerland are not in the majority. In many instances the ratio is but one to three.

These peasants look up curiously as we drive along, and no doubt think that we are favored beings, to whom our luxuries give perfect happiness. And yet the very tourists whom they thus envy may, in a single

A SWISS FARM-HOUSE.

hour, endure more misery and heartache than they in their simplicity and moderate poverty will ever know. Among these people are not found the framers of those hopeless questions: "Is life worth living?" and "Does death end all?" The real destroyers of life's happiness are not a lowly home and manual labor. They are the constant worriments and cares of artificial life,— satiety of pleasures, the overwork of mental powers, and the disenchantment of satisfied desires.

Filled with such thoughts, as we beheld the humble but well-kept and ever picturesque dwellings of the farmers of this valley, I called to mind, as a consoling antidote to one's first natural sympathy with poverty, the story of the sultan who, despite all his wealth and power, was always melancholy. He had been told by his physician that, if he would be cured of all his real or fancied ailments, he must exchange shirts with the first perfectly happy man he could find. Out went his officers in search of such a person.

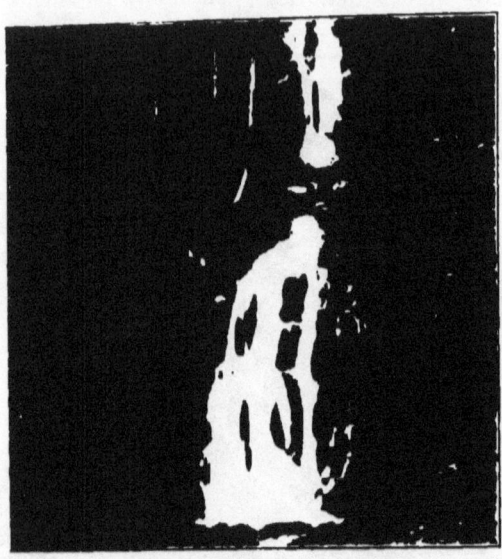

THE GIESSBACH.

The hunt was long and arduous, but finally the fortunate being was found. When he was brought to the sultan, however, it was discovered, alas! that this perfectly happy individual was not the possessor of a shirt.

From Interlaken, every tourist makes a short excursion to one of the best known of Alpine waterfalls, — the Giessbach. Set in a glorious framework of dark trees, it leaves the cliff, one thousand feet above, and in a series of cascades leaps downward to the lake. If this descending torrent were endowed with consciousness, I fancy it would be as wretched in its present state as a captive lion in a cage, continually stared at by a curious multitude. For never was a cascade so completely robbed of liberty and privacy as this. A pathway crosses it repeatedly by means of bridges, and seems to

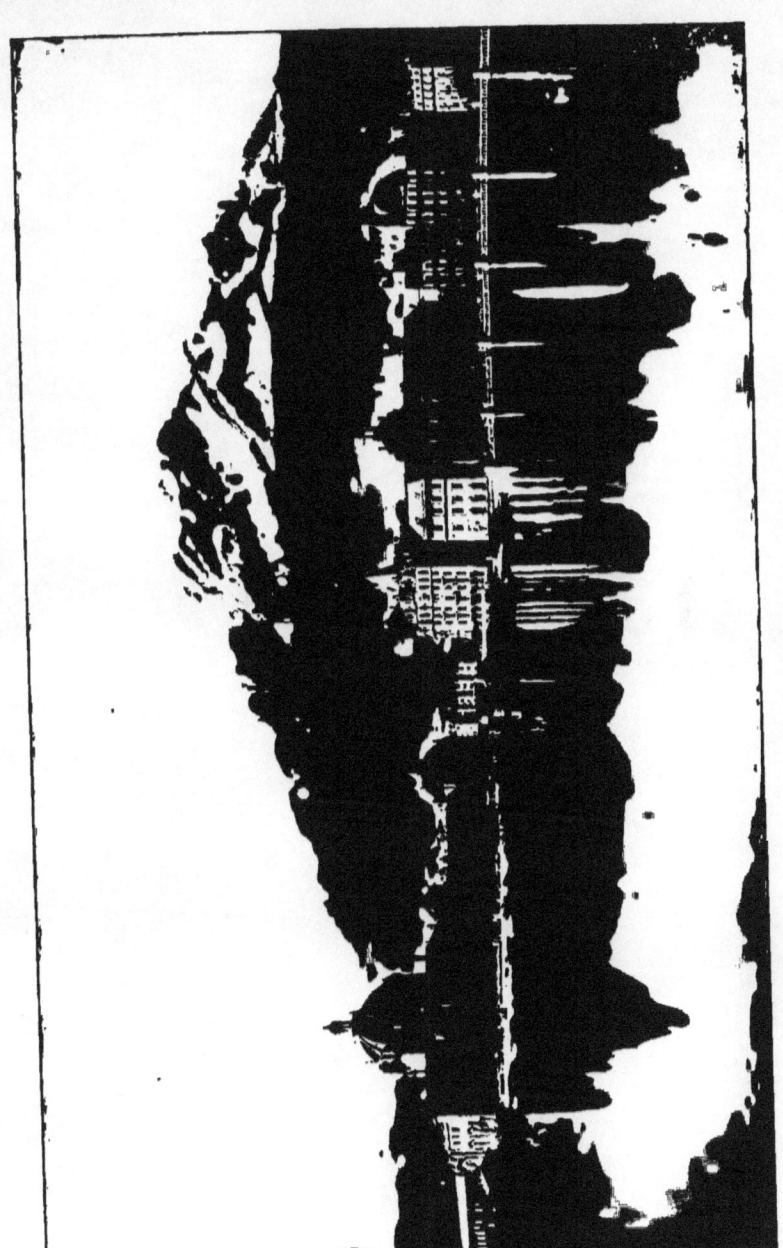

MOUNT PILATE FROM LUCERNE.

bind it to the mountain as with a winding chain. Behind it
are numerous galleries where visitors may view it from the
rear. Arbors and seats are also placed on either side; and thus,
through every hour of the day, people to right of it, people
to left of it, people in rear of it, people in front of it, look
on and wonder.   Even at night it has but little rest; for hardly
have the shadows shrouded it, when it is torn from its obscurity
by torches, calcium lights, and fireworks, which all along
its course reveal it to the admiring crowd in a kaleidoscope
of colors.

Far happier, therefore, seems another waterfall of Switzerland,— the Reichembach; for this is left comparatively undis-
turbed   within
its   mountain
solitude.   Far
off, upon a
mountain crest,
a blue lake, set
like a sapphire
amid surround-
ing   glaciers,
serves as a cra-
dle for this new-
born river.
Thence it
emerges, tim-
idly at first, to
make its way
down to the

THE REICHENBACH.

outer world. With each descent, however, it gains fresh im-
petus and courage. Return is now impossible. The die is
cast. Its fate is now decided. We almost wish that we could
check its course amid this beautiful environment. It will not
find a sweeter or a safer place. Too soon it will be forced to

THE PROMENADE.

bear great burdens, turn countless wheels, and minister to thousands. Then, at the last, will come old Ocean's cold and passionless embrace, in which all its individuality will disappear.

Another portal to this land of mountains, rivaling Interlaken in attractiveness, is Lucerne, reclining peacefully beside its noble lake. I do not know a resting-place in Switzerland which is in all respects so satisfying as this.

Its hotels are among the finest in the world; the town itself is pretty and attractive; and in the foreground is a panorama too varied to become monotonous, too beautiful ever to lose its charm. Mount Pilate and the Rigi guard Lucerne like sentinels, the one on the east, the other on the west, like halting-places for the morning and the evening stars. Directly opposite, upon

THE QUAY, LUCERNE.

the southern boundary of the lake, miles upon miles of snow-capped mountains rise against the sky, as if to indicate the limit of the world.

One of the sentinels of Lucerne, as I have said, is Mount Pilate. Toward this the faces of all tourists turn, as to a huge barom-   eter; for by its cap   of

LUCERNE AND MOUNT PILATE.

clouds Pilate foretells the weather which excursionists must look for. There is hardly need to recall the popular derivation of the mountain's name. It was in olden times believed that Pontius Pilate, in his wanderings through the world, impelled at last by horror and remorse, committed suicide upon its summit. On this account the mountain was considered haunted. At one time the town authorities even forbade people to ascend it on a Friday! But now there is a hotel on the top, and every day in the week, Friday included, a railway train climbs resolutely to the summit, enabling thousands to enjoy every summer a view scarcely to be surpassed in grandeur or extent at any point among the Alps. No allusion to Lucerne would be complete without reference

to that noble product of Thorwaldsen's genius, which, in
more respects than one, is the lion of the place.   It is difficult to imagine a more appropriate memorial than this, of the
fidelity and valor exhibited one hundred years ago by the
Swiss guard, who in defense of Louis XVI laid down their
lives at the opening of the French   Revolu-
tion.   No view does justice to this   famous
statue.   Within a
monstrous niche,
which has been hol-
lowed out of a per-
pendicular cliff, re-
clines, as in some
mountain cave, the
prostrate figure of a
lion, thirty feet in
length.   It is evident
that the animal has
received a mortal
wound.   The handle
of a spear protrudes
from his side.   Yet
even in the agony of
death he guards the
Bourbon shield and
lily, which he has
given his life to de-
fend.   One paw pro-
tects them; his

THE ALPINE ELEVATOR
ON MOUNT PILATE.

drooping head caresses them, and gives to them a
mute farewell.   Beneath the figure, chiseled in the
rock, are the names of the officers murdered by the mob;
while above is the brief but eloquent inscription: "To the
fidelity and bravery of the Swiss."   In the whole world I
do not know of a monument more simple yet impressive.

One of the greatest pleasures of the tourist in Lucerne is to sail out, as he may do at almost any hour of the day, upon its lovely lake. This, in respect to scenery, surpasses all its Alpine rivals. Twenty-three miles in length, it has the form

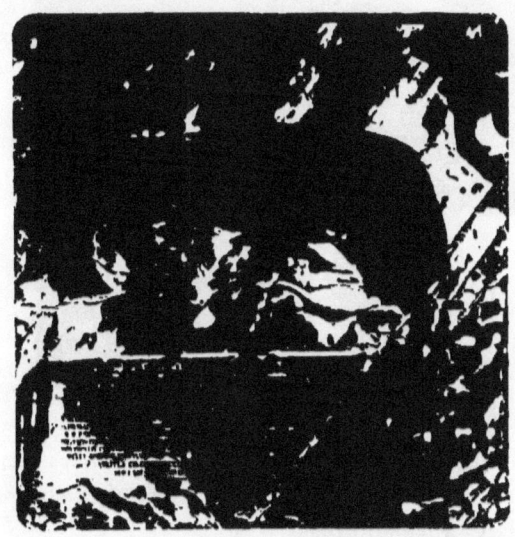

THE LION OF LUCERNE.

of a gigantic cross, each arm of which (when looked upon in the glow of sunset from a neighboring height) seems like a plain

BRUNNEN, ON LAKE LUCERNE.

of gold and lapis-lazuli set in a frame-work of majestic mountains. No tour

MAKING A LANDING.

in Switzerland is complete without a sail upon this fair expanse of water. Hence more than half a million travelers cross it every year during the summer months alone, and tiny steamers are continually visible, cutting their furrows on its smooth, transparent surface, as sharply as a diamond marks a pane of glass.

Moreover, when the boat glides inward toward the shore, one sees that other elements of beauty are not wanting here. Pretty chalets with overhanging roofs; rich pastures, orchards, and gardens,—all these, with numerous villages, succeed each other here for miles, between the lake and the

TELL'S CHAPEL.

MONTREUX.

bold cliffs that rise toward Heaven. Nor is this all. The villages possess a history, since these romantic shores were formerly the stage on which Swiss patriots performed those thrilling scenes immortalized by Schiller in his drama of "William Tell."

In fact, at one point half concealed among the trees is the well-known structure, called Tell's Chapel. It stands upon the spot where, it is said, the hero, springing from the tyrant's boat, escaped the clutches of the Austrian governor. As is well known, doubts have been cast on even the existence of this national chieftain; and yet it is beyond peradventure that a chapel was erected here to his memory as early as the fifteenth century, and only eleven years ago this structure was restored at government expense. Moreover, once a year at least, the people of the neighboring cantons gather here

ALTAR IN TELL'S CHAPEL.

in great numbers to celebrate a festival which has been held by their ancestors for centuries. ~

The little building is certainly well calculated to. awaken patriotism. Appropriate frescoes, representing exploits ascribed to William Tell, adorn the walls; while opposite the doorway is an altar at which religious services are held. How solemn and impressive must the ceremony be, when religious rites are performed in such a historic and picturesque locality in the presence of a reverent multitude! At such a time this

tiny shrine may be considered part of the sublime cathedral
of the mountains, whose columns are majestic trees, whose
stained glass is autumnal foliage, whose anthems are the songs

LAKE LUCERNE BY NIGHT.

of birds, whose requiems are the moaning of the pines, and
whose grand roof is the stupendous arch of the unmeasured
sky, beneath which the snow-clad mountains rise like jeweled
altars, lighted at night, as if with lofty tapers, by the glittering stars.

But to appreciate the beauty of this sheet of water, one
should behold it when its surface is unruffled by a breeze.   En-
amoured of their own beauty, the mountains then look down
into the lake as into an incomparable mirror.   It is an invert-
ed world.   The water is as transparent as the sky.   The very
breezes hold their breath, lest they should mar the exquisite
reflection.   The neighboring peaks display their rugged features in this limpid flood, as if unconscious of the wrinkles
which betray their age.   The pine trees stand so motionless
upon the shore that they appear like slender ferns. - Instinc-

tively we call to mind those graceful lines, supposed to be addressed by such a lake to an adjoining mountain:

> "I lie forever at thy feet,
>   Dear hill with lofty crown;
> My waters smile thy crags to greet,
>   As they look proudly down.
>
> The odor of thy wind-tossed pines
>   Is message sweet to me;
> It makes me dimple with delight,
>   Because it comes from thee.
>
> Thou, lofty, grand, above the world;
>   Its lowly servant, I;
> Yet see, within my sunny depths
>   Is smiling thy blue sky.

FLÜELEN, ON LAKE LUCERNE.

> Thou art so far, and yet how near!
>   For though we are apart,
> I make myself a mirror clear,
>   And hold thee in my heart."

Above this lake itself extends for miles the famous Axenstrasse,—a splendid specimen of engineering skill, cut in the

THE AXENSTRASSE.

solid rock, hundreds of feet above the waves. Yet this is no exceptional thing in Switzerland, and nothing stamps itself more forcibly upon the tourist's mind within this region of the Alps than man's triumphant victory over obstacles, in the formation of its roads. Despite their great cost of construction these prove profitable investments; for the better the roads, the more people will travel over them. Referring to them, some one has prettily said, that by such means the

Swiss transform the silver of their mountain peaks into five franc pieces, and change the golden glow of their sunrises and sunsets into napoleons.

How great the difference between the Switzerland of to-day and that of fifty years

MOUNTAIN GALLERIES.

ago! Where formerly the solitary peasant and his mule picked their precarious way through mud or snow, luxurious

ENGINEERING SKILL.

landaus now roll easily along, on thoroughfares of rock, without a stone or obstruction of any kind to mar their surfaces. Nor is there danger of disaster. Walled in by massive parapets, an accident is here impossible; and in these mighty galleries, hewn from the mountain side itself, the traveler is perfectly secure, although an avalanche may fall or cyclones rage above him.

The Axenstrasse may be said to form a part of that magnificent route from Switzerland to Italy, known as the St. Gotthard. It is, in truth, the king of Alpine roads; resembling a mighty chain which man, the victor, has imposed upon the vanquished Alps,—one end sunk deep in the Italian Lakes, the other guarded by the Lion of Lucerne,—and all the intervening links kept burnished brightly by the hands of trade. True, within the last few years, the carriage-road across the St. Gotthard has been comparatively neglected,

ST. GOTTHARD TUNNEL.

since the longest tunnel in the world has to a great extent replaced it. Tranquil enough this tunnel frequently appears, but I have seen it when great clouds of smoke were pouring out of its huge throat, as from the crater of a great volcano. A strong wind blowing from the south was then, no doubt, clearing this subterranean flue; and I was glad that I had not to breathe its stifling atmosphere, but, on the contrary, seated in a carriage, could lose no portion of the glorious scenery, while drinking in great draughts of the pure mountain air.

Still, whether we travel by the railroad of the St. Gotthard or not, we must not underrate its usefulness, nor belittle the great engineering triumphs here displayed. Its length, too, amazes one, for not only is the principal tunnel nine and a half

VITZNAU ON LAKE LUCERNE.

miles long, but there are fifty-five others on the line, the
total length of which, cut inch by inch out of the solid granite,
is more than twenty-five miles. When one drives over the
mountain by the carriage-road, hour after hour, bewildered by
its cliffs and gorges, it seems impossible that the engineer's
calculations could have been made so perfectly as to enable
labor on the tunnel to be carried on from both ends of it at
the same time. Yet all was planned so well that, on the
28th of February, 1880, the Italian workmen and the Swiss
both met at the designated spot, six thousand feet below the
summit, and there pierced the last thin barrier that remained
between the north and south.

The number of railroad bridges on the St. Gotthard astonished me. Their name is legion. Across them long trains
make their way among the clouds like monster centipedes,
creeping along the mountain-sides, or over lofty viaducts.

Here man's triumph over nature is complete. How puny
seems at first his strength when measured with the wind and

THE ST. GOTTHARD RAILWAY.

avalanche! But mind has proved superior to matter. The ax was made, and at its sturdy stroke the forest yielded up its tribute for the construction of this pathway. The caverns of the earth were also forced to surrender the iron treasured there for ages, and rails were made, along whose glittering lines a crowded train now glides as smoothly as a boat upon the waves. And yet these awful cliffs still scowl so savagely on either

AMSTEG.

side, that the steel rail, which rests upon their shelves of rock, seems often like a thread of fate, by which a thousand lives are held suspended over the abyss.

The volume of freight transported along this route must be enormous. But why should tour-

THE DEVIL'S BRIDGE.

ists (unless compelled by lack of time) consent to be carried through this scenery like a bale of goods, in darkness rather than in daylight? The best way still to cross the Alps is

GÜSCHENEN, ON THE ST. GOTTHARI

to cross them, not to burrow through them. I should certainly advise the traveler to drive from Lake Lucerne over the
St. Gotthard Pass, and then to take the train, if he desires to
do so, on the Italian side, as it emerges from the tunnel.
Thence, in a few brief hours one can embark upon Lake
Como, or see the sunset gild the statue-laden spires of Milan's
cathedral.

The finest scenery on the carriage-road of the St. Gotthard is in a wild ravine, through which the river Reuss
rushes madly. Spanning the torrent in a single arch, is what
is popularly called " The Devil's Bridge." Perhaps I should
say bridges, for there are surely two of them, and though only
the smaller one is attributed to his Satanic Majesty, it is probably by the newer, safer, and more orthodox one that Satan
nowadays, like a prudent devil, prefers to cross. The legend
of this celebrated bridge is extraordinary.

Some centuries ago, the mayor of the canton was one day
in despair because the mountain torrent had swept off every
bridge he had constructed
here. In his

vexation he was rash enough to use
the name of the Devil, as some people
will. Hardly had he uttered the word,
when his door-bell rang, and his servant
brought him a card, on which he read
the words, "Monsieur Satan."

"Show him in," said the mayor.
A gentleman in black made his appearance, and seated himself in an armchair.
The mayor placed his boots upon the
fender; the Devil rested his upon the
burning coals. The subject of the
bridge was broached, and the mayor
finally offered the Devil any sum that
the canton could raise, if he would build
them a bridge which would last one
hundred years. "Bah!" said Satan,
"What need have I of money?" And

taking
with his fin-
gers a red-
hot coal from

PEASANT GIRL.

the fire, he offered it to his companion. The mayor drew back
aghast. "Don't be afraid," said
Satan; and putting the coal in
the mayor's hand, it instantly
became a lump of gold. "Take
it back," said the mayor sadly;
"we are not talking now of
politics!" "You see," said the
Devil, with a smile, "my price
must be something else than
money. If I build this bridge,

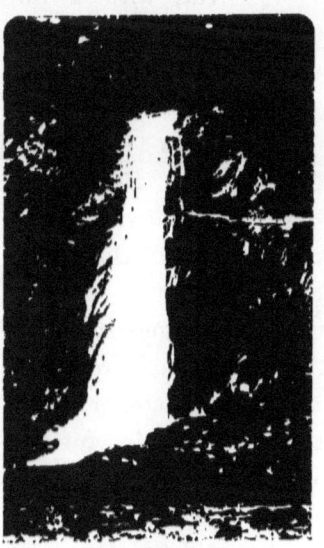

ONE OF THE MANY.

I demand that the first living being that passes over it shall be mine." "Agreed!" said the mayor. The contract was soon signed. "Au revoir!" said the Devil. "Au plaisir!" said the mayor; and Satan went his way.

Early next morning the mayor himself hurried to the spot, eager to see if Satan had fulfilled his contract. The bridge was completed, and there sat Satan, swinging his legs over the stream and waiting for his promised soul. "What," he exclaimed, as he espied the mayor, "do you unselfishly resign *your* soul to me?" "Not much," replied the mayor, proceeding to untie a bag which he had brought. "What's that?" cried Satan. There was a wild yell, and instantly a big black cat, with a tin pan tied to its tail, rushed over the bridge as if

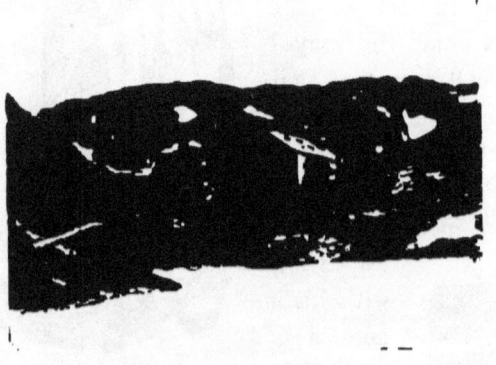

HOSPICE ST. BERNARD AND LAKE.

ten thousand dogs were after it. "There is your 'first living being,'" cried the mayor. "Catch him!" Satan was furious, but acknowledged that he had been outwitted and retired,—contenting himself with making the air of the ravine quite sulphurous with his remarks about home!

Although the St. Gotthard may be the grandest of all Alpine passes, the most historic of them is that of Mount St. Bernard. Some years ago, on the last day of October, I left the village of Martigny, which is the starting-point for the ascent, and, several hours later, as night came creeping up the Alps, found myself upon the famous pass, at a place already higher than our own Mt. Washington, but still two thousand

feet below my destination,—the monastery. Through various causes our party had been delayed, and now with the approach of night a snow-storm swept our path with fearful vio-
lence. Those who have never seen a genuine Alpine storm
can hardly comprehend its reckless fury. The light snow was

WHERE AVALANCHES FALL.

whirled and scattered,
like an ocean of spray,
over all things. A thou-
sand needles of ice
seemed to pierce our
skin. Drifts sprang up
in our path, as if by
magic. The winds
howled like unchained
demons through the jagged gorges, and a horrible feeling
of isolation made our hearts falter with a sickening sense
of helplessness. As mine was an October experience, I
shudder to think of what a genuine winter's storm must
be. For, as it was, we were all speedily numb with cold,

blinded by the whirling snow, and deafened by the roaring wind, which sometimes drowned our loudest shouts to one another.

Up and still up we rode, our poor mules plunging through the snow, our fingers mechanically holding the reins, which felt like icicles within our grasp, our guides rubbing their well-nigh frozen hands, but, fortunately—most fortunately—never becoming confused as to the way.

At length I saw, or thought I saw, through the blinding snow, one of a group of buildings. I chanced to be the foremost in our file of snow-bound travelers, and shouting, "Here it is at last," I hastened toward the structure. No light was visible. No voice responded to my call for help. I pounded on the door and called again. No answer came; but at that

A SWISS OSSUARY.

moment I felt my arm grasped roughly by my guide. "In Heaven's name," he said, "do not jest on such a night as this."

"Jest!" I rejoined, with chattering teeth, "I have no wish to jest — I am freezing. Where is the boasted hospitality of your lazy monks? Shout! Wake them up!"

"They will not wake," replied the guide. "Why not?" I cried; and beating the door again, I called at the top of my voice: "Au secours! Réveillez-vous! Are you all dead in here?"

"Yes," replied the guide.

It was now my turn to stare

A CORRIDOR IN THE HOSPICE.

at him. "What do you mean?" I faltered. "What—what does this house contain?" "Corpses," was the reply.

It was clear to me in a moment. I had mistaken the dead-house for the house of shelter! In fancy I could see the ghastly spectacle within, where bones of travelers whiten on through centuries in an atmosphere whose purity defies decay.

But, almost simultaneously with his other words, I heard my guide exclaim: "If you too would not join their number, *en avant, en avant, vite, vite!*" Then, seizing the bridle of my mule, he urged me toward the monastery. A few moments more and we arrived within its sheltering walls. One of the brothers helped me to dismount, and led me up the stone steps of the Hospice. And then, how blessed was our reception! How warm the fire blazing on the ample hearth!

DOGS OF ST. BERNARD.

How good the hot soup and wine instantly brought us by the kind friars! How comforting the thought of our surroundings, as the baffled storm beat against the frost-covered windows, and seemed to shriek with rage at being cheated of its victims!

Never, while memory lasts, shall I cease to remember with love and gratitude those noble-hearted brothers of the St. Bernard.

Next morning the storm had cleared away; yet even in pleasant weather it is difficult to imagine anything more dreary than the situation of this monastery, locked thus in snow and ice, and sentineled by savage peaks, eight thousand feet above the sea. Even the pond adjoining it is gloomy from its contrast to all other lakes. Its waters are too cold for any kind of fish, and therefore fail to attract hither any kind of bird. Animal life has fallen off in mak-

BROTHERS OF ST. BERNARD.

ing the ascent. Man and the dog alone have reached the summit.

It was with admiration that I looked upon the self-sacrificing heroes who reside here. What praise can be too high for these devoted men, who say farewell to parents and to friends, and leave the smiling vales of Switzer- land and Italy to live upon this glacial height? Few of them can endure the hardship and exposure of the situation longer than eight years, and then, with broken health, they return (perhaps to die) to the milder climate of the valleys. During the long winter which binds them here with icy chains for nine months of the year, they give themselves to the noble work of rescuing, often amid terrible exposure, those who are then obliged to cross the pass. In this they are aided by their famous dogs, which, like themselves, shrink from no danger, and in their courage and intelligence rival the masters they so bravely serve. The travelers whom they receive in winter are not the rich, whose heavy purses might recompense them for their

OLD CITY GATE, BASLE.

toil. They are mostly humble peasants, unable to give more compensation than the outpouring of a grateful heart. But there will come a day when these brave men will have their full reward; when He, who with unerring wisdom weighs all motives and all deeds, will say to them: "Inasmuch as ye have done it unto one of the least of these my brethren, ye have done it unto Me."

One of the most attractive of all the pleasure resorts in Switzerland is the lovely Vale of Chamonix. The first view one obtains of it, in coming over the mountains from Martigny, is superb. Three monstrous glaciers, creeping out from their

CHAMONIX AND MOUNT BLANC.

icy lairs, lie beneath ice-fringed buttresses of snow, like glittering serpents watching for a favorable chance to seize and swallow their prey. Looking across the valley at them, it is true, they seem quite harmless; but in reality, such glaciers are the mighty wedges which have for ages carved these mountains into shape, and are still keeping them apart in solitary grandeur. What from a distance seems a little bank of snow is probably a wall of ice, one hundred feet in height. What look like wrinkles are crevasses of an unknown depth; and the seeming puff of smoke which one at times discerns upon them, is really a tremendous

MER DE GLACE FROM HOTEL MONTAVERDE.

APPALLING PRECIPICES.

avalanche of snow and ice. Of the three glaciers which descend into the Vale of Chamonix, the one most frequently visited by tourists is the Mer de Glace. It is well called the "Sea of Ice," for its irregular surface looks precisely like a mass of tossing waves which have been crystallized when in their wildest agitation. To right and left, the ice is partially concealed by rocks and earth, which have been ground off from the adjacent mountain-sides, or which have fallen there, as the result of avalanches. Sometimes huge boulders are discernible, tossed here and there like nut-shells, the rocky *débris* of ages.

What is there more suggestive of mysterious

ZÜRICH, WITH DISTANT ALPS.

power than a frozen cataract like this? Apparently as cold
and motionless as death, it nevertheless is moving downward
with a slow, resistless march, whose progress can be accurately
traced from
day to day;
so accurately,
indeed, that
objects lost
to-day in one
of these cre-
vasses may be

confidently
looked for at
the glacier's
terminus after
a certain num-
ber of years.
Forever nour-
ished on the
heights, for-

FROZEN CATARACTS.

ever wasting in the valleys, these glaciers are the moving
mysteries of the upper world; vast, irresistible, congealed pro-
cessions, — the frozen reservoirs of rivers that glide at last
from their reluctant arms in a mad haste to reach the sea.

"Perennial snow, perennial stream,
Perennial motion, all things seem;
Nor time, nor space will ever show
The world that was an hour ago."

When we examine any portion of a glacier's surface,
we find abundant evidence of its motion. It has been forced

into a million strange, distorted shapes, many of which are larger than the grandest cathedrals man has ever framed. Between them are vast chasms of unknown depth. As it descends thus, inch by inch, obedient to the pressure from

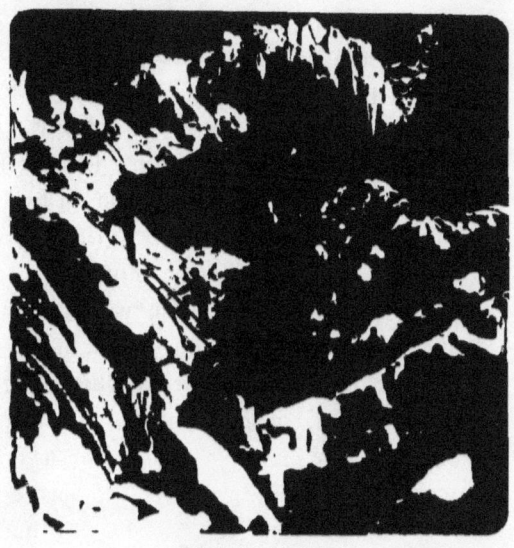

CROSSING A GLACIER.

above, it flings its frigid waves to the right and left, close to the orchards and the homes of man. It is the ghastly synonym of death in life; for here a man may swing the scythe or gather flowers, while a hundred yards away his brother may be perishing in a crevasse!

To really understand a glacier one must venture out upon its icy flood. One day

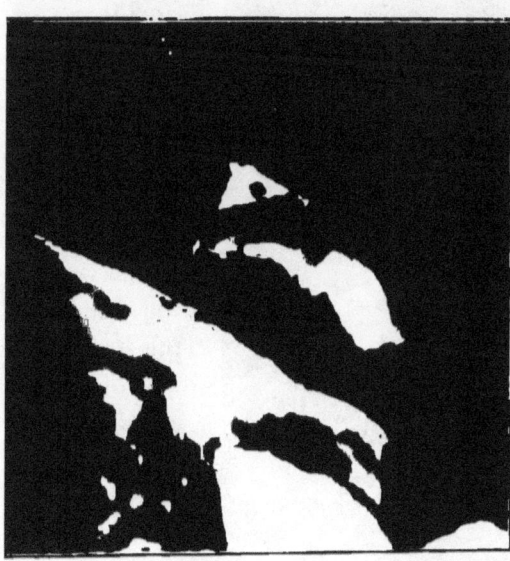

A PERILOUS SEAT.

while on the Mer de Glace, I was (as usual in such expeditions) preceded and followed by a guide, to both of whom I was attached by a stout rope. On that occasion one thing impressed me greatly. It was a strange sound, called by the guides "brullen," or growling, which is in reality the mysterious moaning of the glacier, caused by the rending asunder of huge blocks of ice in its slow, grinding descent.

At times it seemed to me impossible to proceed, but the experienced guide who led the way laughed at my fears; and finally, to increase my confidence, actually entered one of the appalling caverns of the glacier, which like the jaws of some huge polar bear, seemed capable of closing with dire consequences. For a few minutes he remained over- seated beneath a mass of overhanging ice, apparently as calm as I was apprehensive for his safety. No accident occurred, and yet my fears were not unfounded. For though there is a fascination in thus venturing beneath the frozen billows of a glacier, there may be treachery in its siren loveliness. Huge blocks of ice

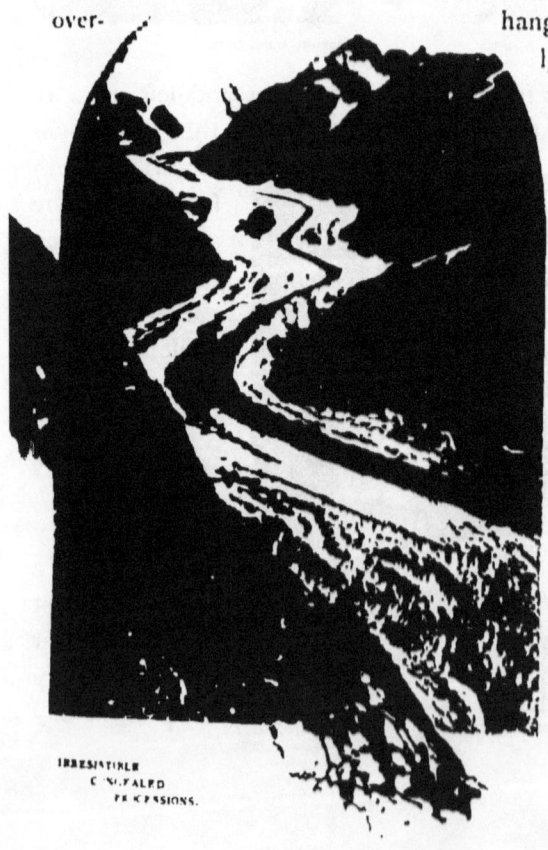

CHAMONIX AND MONT BLANC.

frequently fall without the slightest warning, and many a reckless tourist has thus been killed, or perhaps maimed for life.

On entering the little town of Chamonix, the tourist sees in front of one of the hotels a group in bronze

MONT BLANC FROM CHAMONIX.

that rivets his attention and awakens thought. It represents the famous guide, Balmat, who first ascended Mont Blanc in 1786, enthusiastically pointing out the path of victory to the Swiss scientist, De Saussure, who had for years been offering a reward to any one who should discover a way to reach the summit.

The face of the brave conqueror of Mont Blanc and that of the distinguished scholar are both turned toward the monarch of the Alps. Instinctively the traveler also looks in that direction.

It is a memorable moment when one gazes for the first time upon

DE SAUSSURE AND BALMAT.

Mont Blanc. We understand at once the reason for its
being called preëminently the "White Mountain." The
title was bestowed upon it because of the magnificent snow-
white mantle which it wears, at a height of almost sixteen
thousand feet. Probably no other mountain in the world
has so towered up on the horizon of our imaginations. Long
before we have actually seen it, we have repeated Byron's
words:

> "Mount Blanc is the monarch of mountains;
> They crowned him long ago,
> On a throne of rocks, in a robe of clouds,
> With a diadem of snow."

At once a strong desire seizes us to explore those boundless fields of crystal clearness, and yet we shrink from all the
toil and danger thus involved. But, suddenly, as our gaze
returns to earth, we find a means of making the ascent without fatigue — the telescope!

The placard suspended from it tells us that some tourists
are actually struggling toward the summit. The chances are
that they will return in safety; for the ascent of Mont Blanc,
which Balmat made with so much difficulty, has now been
reduced to a system. Yet after all, this Alpine climbing
is a dangerous business. It is pathetic, for example, to

A MOUNTAIN MAUSOLEUM.

recall the fate of poor Balmat himself. Despite his long experience, even *he* lost his life at last by falling over a precipice. Only his statue is in Chamonix; his body lies in an immense abyss, four hundred feet in depth, where falling masses of rock and ice are constantly increasing his vast mausoleum, and the continual thunder of the avalanche seems like the mountain's exultation at its conqueror's destruction.

CLIMBERS IN SIGHT.

Availing ourselves of the telescope, we watch with ease and comfort the actual climbers on Mont Blanc. By this time they have bound themselves together with a rope, which in positions of peril is the first requisite of safety. For one must always think of safety on these mountains. With all their beauty and grandeur, they have sufficient capability for cruelty to make the blood run cold. They have no mercy in them; no sympathy for the warm hearts beating so near their surfaces. They submit passively to conquest, so long as man preserves a cool head and sure footing. But let him make one false step; let his brain swim, his heart fail, his hand falter, and they will hurl him from their icy slopes, or tear him to pieces on their jagged tusks, while in the roar of the avalanche is heard their demoniac laughter.

But following the tourists still farther up the mountain, we look with dismay at one of the icy crests along which they must presently advance. Not a charming place for a promenade, truly! Here it would seem that one should use an alpen-stock rather as a balancing-pole than as a staff. It is enough to make even a Blondin falter and retire. For, coated with a glare of ice, and bordered on either side by an abyss, the slightest misstep would inevitably send one shooting down this glittering slope to certain death in one of the vast folds of Mont Blanc's royal mantle.

Lifting now the telescope a little higher, we note another difficulty which mountain-climbers frequently encounter. For here they have come face to face with a perpendicular wall of ice which they must climb, or else acknowledge a defeat. The bravest, therefore, or the strongest, cuts with his ax a sort of stairway in this crystal barrier, and, making his way upward by this perilous route, lowers a rope and is rejoined by his companions. Imagine doing this in the teeth of such wind and cold as must often be met with on these crests!

ALPINE PERILS.

THE WEISSBACH.

Think of it,
when a gale is
tearing off the
upper snow,
and driving it
straight into
the face in
freezing spray
like a shower of
needles; when
the gloves are
coated with ice,
and alpen-
stocks slide
through them,
slippery as eels;

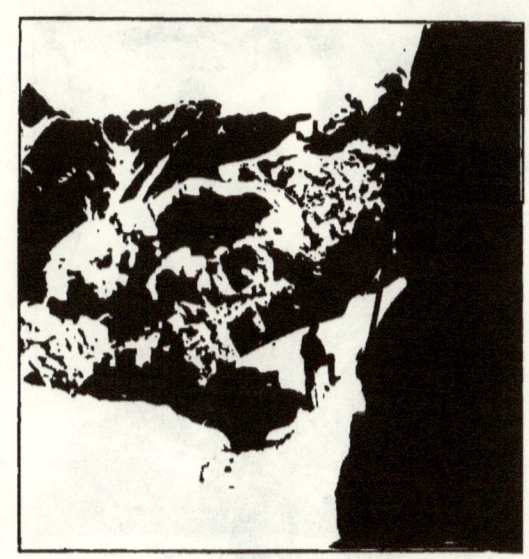

AN ICE WALL.

and when the ice-bound rocks tear off the skin from the half-
frozen fingers of the man who clings to them for life!

I know it is customary now to laugh at any dangers on
Mont Blanc; and yet a terrible disaster took place there no
longer ago than 1870.

In the month of September of that year, a party of eleven
(including two Americans) started to climb the mountain.
Near the summit a frightful tempest burst upon them. The
guides no longer recognized the way, and, unable to return or
find shelter, the entire party perished. The bodies of five
were recovered. In the pocket of one of them (an American
from Baltimore) were found these words, written to his wife:
" 7th of September, evening. We have been for two days
on Mont Blanc in a terrific hurricane. We have lost our way,
and are now at an altitude of fifteen thousand feet. I have
no longer any hope. We have nothing to eat. My feet are
already frozen, and I have strength enough only to write
these words. Perhaps they will be found and given to you.

HUTS OF SHELTER ON MONT BLANC.

Farewell; I trust that we shall meet in heaven!"

But such a mountain as Mont Blanc can rarely be ascended in a single day. Two days are generally given to the task. On the evening of the first day its would-be conquerors reach, at a height of ten thousand feet, a desolate region called the Grands Mulets. Here on some savage-looking rocks are two small cabins. One is intended for a kitchen, the other for a sleeping-room;

WHERE SEVERAL ALPINE CLIMBERS REST.

that is, if one can sleep in such a place; for what an excitement there must be in passing a night at this great altitude! The distant stars gleam in the frosty air with an unwonted brilliancy and splendor. The

A SEA OF CLOUDS.

wind surges against the cliffs with the full, deep boom of the sea; while the silence in the unmeasurable space above is awe-inspiring.

But, on the morrow, the glorious view repays one for a night of sleeplessness. At first one looks apparently upon a

CAVERNOUS JAWS.

shoreless ocean, whose rolling billows seem now white, now opalescent, in the light of dawn. Then, one by one, the various mountain peaks appear like islands rising from the sea. At last, these waves of vapor sink slowly downward through the valleys, and disappear in full retreat before the god of day. But till they vanish, the traveler could suppose that he had here survived the deluge of the world, and was watching its huge shrouded corpse at his feet.

Between the Grands Mulets and the summit, Mont Blanc makes three tremendous steps, from eight hundred to one thousand feet in height, and between these are several fright-ful chasms, so perilous that on beholding them we catch our breath. There is something peculiarly horrible in these cre-vasses, yawning gloomily, day and night, as if with a never-satisfied hunger. A thousand—nay ten thousand—men in their cavernous jaws would not constitute a mouthful. They are even more to be dreaded than the avalanche; for the path of the avalanche is usually known; but these crevasses fre-quently hide their black abysses under deceitful coverlets of snow, luring unwary travelers to destruction. Nevertheless the avalanche is in certain places an ever-present danger. Mountains of snow stand toppling on the edge of some stu-pendous cliff, apparently waiting merely for the provocation of a human voice, intruding on their solitude, to start upon their awful plunge. The world well knows the fate of those who have been caught in such a tor- rent of de- struc- tion.

BASLE: THE BRIDGE AND CATHEDRAL.

A BRIDGE OF ICE.

"No breath for words! no time for thought! no play
 For eager muscle! guides, companions, all
 O'ermastered in the unconquerable drift,
 In Nature's grasp held powerless, atoms
 Of her insensate frame, they fared as leaves
 In the dark rapid of November gales,
 Or sands sucked whirling into fell simooms;
 One gasp for breath, one strangled, bitter cry,
 And the cold, wild snow closed smothering in,
 And cast their forms about with icy shrouds,
 And crushed the life out, and entombed them there,—
 Nobler than kings Egyptian in their pyramids,
 Embalmèd in the mountain mausoleum,
 And part of all its grand unconsciousness
 Forever.
              Its still dream resumed the Mount;
 The sun his brightness kept; for unto them
 The living men are naught, and naught the dead,
 No more than snows that slide or stones that roll."

Finally, these and all other dangers being past, the
wearied but exultant climbers reach the summit of Mont Blanc,

ENGLISH CHURCH, CHAMONIX.

—that strangely silent, white, majestic dome, so pure and spotless in its lofty elevation beneath the stars. To watch this scene from the Vale of Chamonix, when the great sovereign of our solar system sinks from sight, leaving upon Mont Blanc his crown of gold, is an experience that will leave one only with one's life. The concentrated refulgence on that solitary dome is so intense that one is tempted to believe that the glory of a million sunsets, fading from all other summits of the Alps, has been caught and imprisoned here. We know that sun will rise again; but who, in such a place, can contemplate unmoved the death of Day?

> "The night has a thousand eyes,
>   And the day but one;
> Yet the light of the bright world dies,
>   With the dying sun!
>
> The mind has a thousand eyes,
>   And the heart but one;
> Yet the light of a whole life dies,
>   When love is done."

MOUNTAIN CLIMBERS.

One singular experience of Alpine travel is indelibly impressed upon my memory.   It occurred on my passage of the

Gemmi into the valley of the Rhone. The Gemmi Pass is no magnificent highway like the St. Gotthard, macadamized and smooth and carefully walled in by parapets of stone. It is for miles a rough and dangerous bridle-path, the edge of which

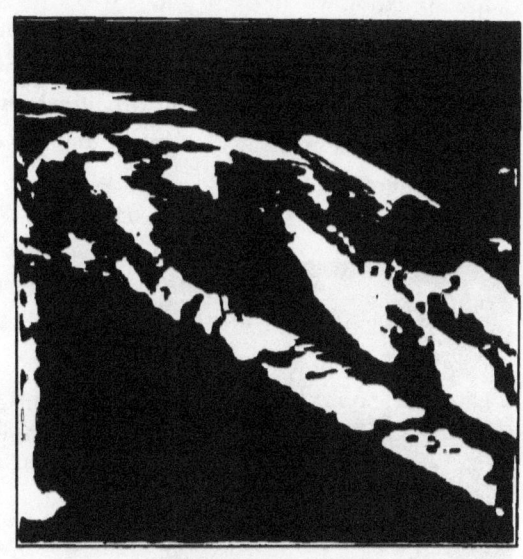

THE BIRTH-PLACE OF AVALANCHES.

is sometimes decorated with a flimsy rail, but often has not even that apology for safety.   One can thus readily believe that, like the Jordan, the Gemmi is emphatically "a hard road to travel."   At all events I found it so, especially as I crossed it early in the season, before the winter's ravages had

MOUNTAIN MULES.

been repaired. Since I was at the time suffering from a temporary lameness, I could walk but little. With this road dates my first acquaintance with a mule,—an intimacy that will never be forgotten!   All day long that memorable beast would never for one instant change his gait, nor was the monotony of his dreadful walk once broken by a trot. My only consolation was in the thought that if the beast did change it, my neck, as well as the monotony, would probably be broken. Thus, hour after hour, I kept moving on and up, my knees forced wide apart by this great, lumbering wedge, until I felt like a colossal wish-bone, and as though I should be bow-legged for the rest of my life.

Nor was this all; for, as the day wore on, the mule took

A FRAIL PARAPET.

special pains to make my blood run cold by a variety of acrobatic feats, which might have made a chamois faint with vertigo. For example, wherever a rail was lacking in the crazy fence, he would deliberately fill the space with his own body and mine, walking so dangerously near the brink, that half my form would be suspended over the abyss! Of course, the moment it was passed, I laughed or scolded, as most travelers do; yet, after all, in such cases we never know how great the peril may have been. A little stone, a clod of earth, a movement in the nick of time — these are sometimes the only things which lie between one and the great Unknown, and hinder one from prematurely solving the mysterious problem of existence.

Nevertheless, on the fearful precipices for which the Gemmi is noted, one may be pardoned for being a trifle nervous. At certain points the bridle-path so skirts the chasm that one false step would land the fragments of your body on the rocks a thousand feet below; while, on the other side, the mountain towers up abrupt and bare, with scarce a shrub or tree to cling to or console the dizzy traveler. My flesh creeps now to think of

UP AMONG THE CLOUDS.

some of these places; and in the same space of time I think I never repented of so many sins, as during that passage of the

ON THE GEMMI.

Gemmi. At length, however, the climax seemed reached; for at the brink of one abyss the path appeared to end. I cautiously advanced to the edge and looked over. It was a fearful sight, for here the mountain falls away to a sheer depth of sixteen hundred feet, and the plumb-line might drop to that full length without encountering any obstacle.

When Alexander Dumas came to this place, and (unprepared for what he was to see) looked down from the brink of the stupendous precipice, he fell back unconscious; and afterward, while making the descent, his teeth so chattered with nervousness, that he placed his folded handkerchief between

LEUK.

them. Yet when, on reaching the valley, he removed it, he found it had been cut through and through as with a razor. I cannot, certainly, lay claim to nervousness like that; but I could sympathize with one of our fellow-countrymen, against whose name on the hotel register I next day saw these words: "Thank God, we don't raise such hills as these in the State of New York!"

At the other side of the Gemmi, and almost at the base of these gigantic cliffs, there lies a little village. When I stood on the precipice above it, I thought that a pebble hurled thence from my hand would fall directly on its roofs; but in reality their distance from the cliffs was greater than it seemed. This village is the celebrated Leuk, whose baths have now acquired a world-wide reputation. Leuk has, however, this misfortune: so many strangers come here now to bathe, that

many of the in-
habitants them-
selves think that
they can dis-
pense with the
luxury.

I never shall
forget the baths
of Leuk. Shades
of the Mermaids!
what a sight they
presented. In a
somewhat shab-
by hall, contain-
ing great com-
partments of hot

PARBOILED PATIENTS.

water, I saw a multitude of heads — long-haired and short-
haired, light and dark, male and female — bobbing about like

A LOW BRIDGE.

buoys adorned with
sea-weed. A fine
chance this to study
physiognomy, pure
and simple. In front
of these amphibious
creatures were float-
ing tables, upon
which they could
eat, drink, knit,
read, and even play
cards to pass away
the time. As these
waters are chiefly
used for skin dis-
eases, one might

suppose that each bather would prefer a separate room; but no, in this case "misery loves company." The length of time which one must remain soaking in these tanks of hot water makes solitary bathing unendurable.

I asked one of these heads how long it had to float here daily. The mouth opened just above the water's edge and answered: "Eight hours, Monsieur; four before luncheon, and four before dinner; and, as after each bath we have to spend an hour in bed, ten hours a day are thus consumed."

It may seem incredible, but I assure the reader that some of these parboiled bathers actually sleep while in these tanks. I, myself, saw a head drooped backward as though severed from the body. Its eyes were closed; its mouth was slightly open; and from the nose a mournful sound came forth at intervals, which told me that the man was snoring. Before him, half-supported by the little table, half-bedraggled in the flood, was a newspaper.

Bending over the rail, I read the title. Poor man! I no longer wondered that he slept. Those who have read the ponderous sheet will understand its soporific effect. It was a copy of the London *Times*.

After the baths of Leuk and the stupendous precipices of the Gemmi, it is a pleasure to approach a less imposing but more beautiful part of Switzerland, — Geneva and its lake. The bright, cream-colored buildings of the one present a beautiful

A WAITRESS AT LEUK.

NATIONAL MONUMENT — GENEVA.

contrast to the other's deep blue waves. Next to Stockholm and Naples, Geneva has, I think, the loveliest situation of any city in Europe. Curved, crescent-like, around the southwest

THE RHONE AT GENEVA.

corner of the lake, the river Rhone with arrowy swiftness cleaves it into two parts, thus furnishing the site for all the handsome quays and bridges which unite the various sections of the town.

What a surprising change has taken place in the appearance of the river Rhone since it first poured its waters into

GENEVA—THE BRUNSWICK MONUMENT.

Lake Geneva at its other extremity, forty-five miles away! There it is muddy, dark, and travel-stained from its long journey down the valley. But here it has become once more as pure as when it left its cradle in the glaciers. Its sojourn in the lake has given it both beauty and increased vitality; and as it starts again upon its course and darts out from Geneva with renewed strength and speed, its waters are superbly blue and clear as crystal.

As it emerges from the lake, a sharp-pointed island confronts the rapid stream, as if awaiting its advance. Its station here before the city resembles that of some fair maid of honor who precedes a queen. It is called Rousseau's Island, in honor of the famous man whose birth the

ROUSSEAU'S ISLAND.

city claims. Geneva certainly should be grateful to him, for it was he who first made this fair lake renowned in literature, and called to it the attention of the world. In fact, he did almost as much to render famous this enchanting spot, as Scott did for the region of the Trosachs. Appropriately, therefore, a fine bronze statue of Rousseau has been erected on the island, the figure looking up the lake, like the presiding genius of the place.

One can with both pleasure and profit spend a fortnight in Geneva. Its well-kept and luxurious hotels all front upon the

quays, and from your windows there (as from the Grand Hotel
in Stockholm) you look upon an ever-varying panorama—a
charming combination of metropolitan and aquatic life.
Boats come and go at frequent intervals, accompanied by the
sound of music. The
long perspectives of the
different bridges, full of
animated life, afford

GENEVA—RUE DE MONT BLANC.

perpetual entertainment; while, in
dull weather, the attractive shops,
in some respects unrivaled in the
whole of Europe, tempt you, be-
yond your power to resist, to purchase music-
boxes or enameled jewelry. After all, one's greatest pleasure
here is to embark upon the lake itself. This famous body of
water forms a beautiful blue crescent, forty-five miles in
length and eight in breadth. Tyndall declared that it had
the purest natural water ever analyzed; Voltaire called it the
"First of Lakes;" Alexander Dumas compared it to the
Bay of Naples; while Victor Hugo, Lamartine, and Byron
have given it boundless praise in their glowing verse. It
has been estimated that should the lake henceforth receive

no further increase, while having still the river
Rhone for its outlet, it would require ten years to
exhaust its volume. It might be likened, therefore, to a little inland
sea. In fact, a pretty
legend says that the
ocean-deity, Neptune,
came one day to see
Lake Leman, and, en-
raptured with its fresh
young beauty, gave to
it, on departing, his
likeness in miniature.
Moreover, it has another charm
—that of historical association.

INNS AT WORK—GENEVA.

Its shores have been the residence of men of genius. Both
history and poetry have adorned its banks with fadeless wreaths
of love and fame. Each hill that rises softly from its waves is
crowned with some distinguished memory. Byron has often
floated on its surface; and here he wrote some portions of
"Childe Harold," which will be treasured to the end of time.

LAKE GENEVA.

CASTLE OF CHILLON.

The poet Shelley narrowly escaped drowning in its waters.
At one point Madame de Staël lived in exile; another saw
Voltaire for years maintaining here his intellectual court;
while at Lausanne, upon the memorable night which he
has well described,   Gibbon concluded
his immortal   work, "The
Decline   and Fall

LAUSANNE, ON LAKE GENEVA.

of the Roman Empire." But of all portions of Lake Leman,
that which charms one most is the neighborhood of Montreux
and Vevey, and the historic Castle of Chillon. A poet's
inspiration has made this place familiar to the world. No
English-speaking traveler, at least, can look upon these towers,

rising from the waves, without recalling Byron's "Prisoner of Chillon," and reciting its well-known
lines:

"Lake Leman lies by Chillon's walls:
A thousand feet in depth below
Its massy waters meet and flow;
Thus much the fathom-line was sent
From Chillon's snow-white battlement."

This time-worn structure boasts
a thousand years of story and romance. In fact, more than a thousand years ago, Louis le Débonnaire
imprisoned here a traitor to his king.

WHILE THE STEAMER WAITS.

Here, also, five centuries ago, hundreds of Jews were tortured,
and then buried alive, on the infamous suspicion of poisoning
the wells of   Europe. But
of all   the

CASTLE AND CATHEDRAL, LAUSANNE.

memories which cluster
round its walls the most
familiar is that of Bonnivard, the Swiss patriot, who
languished for six years in its

dark dungeon, till he was released by the efforts of his enthusiastic countrymen.   During those gloomy years of captivity his jailers heard from him no cry and no complaint, save when some tempest swept the lake. Then, when the wind moaned, as if in sympathy, around the towers, and waves dashed high against the walls, they could distinguish sobs and cries, prov-

ON THE SHORE.

ing that, when apparently alone with God, the captive sought to give his burdened soul relief.

> "Chillon! thy prison is a holy place,
>   And thy sad floor an altar — for 't was trod
> Until his very steps have left a trace
>   Worn, as if thy cold pavement were a sod,
> By Bonnivard! — May none those marks efface!
>   For they appeal from tyranny to God."

When finally his liberators burst into his cell, they found him pale and shadow-like, still chained to the column around which he had walked so many years.   A hundred voices cried to him at once: "Bonnivard, you are free!"   The prisoner slowly rose, and his first question was: "And Geneva?" "Free, also!" was the answer.

One night, some eighty years ago, a little boat came toward this castle, leaving behind it in its course a furrow

silvered by the moon. . As it reached the shore, there sprang
from it a man enveloped in a long black cloak, which almost

CASTLE OF CHILLON.

hid his feet from
view. A close
observer would
have seen, how-
ever, that he
limped slightly.
He asked to see
the historic dun-
geon, and lin-
gered there an
hour alone.

When he had gone, they found on the stone column to which
Bonnivard had been chained a new name carved. The traveler

sees it there to-
day. It is the
name of Byron.

There is in
Switzerland a
village superior
even to Chamo-
nix in grandeur
of location, dom-
inated by a
mountain more
imposing even
than Mont
Blanc. The
town is Zermatt;
the mountain is
the Matterhorn.

THE DUNGEON OF CHILLON.

As we approach it, we discern only a tiny part of its environment; but could we soar aloft with the eagle, and take a

THE MATTERHORN EXACTED SPEEDY VENGEANCE.

bird's-eye view of it, the little village would appear to have
been caught in a colossal trap of rock and ice.   There is, in
fact, no path to
it, save over dan-
gerous passes,
or through a
narrow cleft in
the encircling
mountains, down
which a river
rushes with im-
petuous fury;
while, watching

HISTORIC WATERS.

over it, like some divinely-stationed sentinel, rises the awful
Matterhorn, the most unique and imposing mountain of the

ZERMATT.

Alps. No view
can possibly
do it justice;
yet, anticipate
what you will,
it is here im-
possible to be
disappointed.
Though every
other object
of the world
should fail, the
Matterhorn
must stir the
heart of the
most unim-
pressive trav-
eler. Not only does its icy wedge pierce the blue air at a
height of fifteen thousand feet above the sea, but its gaunt,

tusk-like form emerges from the surrounding glaciers with almost perpendicular sides, four thousand feet in height. It is a mani- festation of the power of the Deity, beside which all the works of man dwindle to insignificance. I never grew accustomed to this, as to other mountains. No matter when I gazed upon its sharp-cut edges and its ice-bound rocks, I felt, as when I first beheld it, completely

SAFE FROM
MOUNTAIN PERILS.

overpowered by its magnitude. The history of this colossal pyramid is as tragic as its grim form is awe-inspiring. The mountain is known as the " Fiend of the Alps." Year after

FALLS OF THE RHINE, SCHAFFHAUSEN.

year it had been
luring to itself,
with fearful fas-
cination, scores
of brave men
who longed to
scale its appal-
ling cliffs. Over
its icy pedestal,
—up its precip-
itous sides, —
yes, even to its
naked shoul-
ders, baffled
and wistful
mountaineers

THE FIEND OF THE ALPS.

struggled in vain. Upon its perpendicular rocks several men
had all but perished; but the warnings were unheeded. At

length, after per-
sistent efforts
for eleven years,
the famous Eng-
lish mountain-
climber, Whym-
per, gained the
summit. But in
return for the
humiliation of
this conquest the
Matterhorn ex-
acted speedy
vengeance.

As the suc-
cessful party,

MOONLIGHT ON THE MATTERHORN.

consisting of four Englishmen and three guides, elated by
their victory, were just beginning their descent, one of them
slipped, knocking a guide completely off his feet and dragging
his companions after him, since all were bound together by a
rope. Four of them hung an instant there, head downward,
between earth and heaven. The other three clung desperately
to the icy   crags, and
would   have

BERNE.

rescued them, had not the rope
between them broken. There was
a fearful cry — a rush of falling
bodies. Then Whymper and two guides
found themselves clinging to the rocks, and
looking into each other's haggard faces, pale as
death. The others had fallen over the precipice — nearly
four thousand feet — to the ice below!

> "One moment stood they, as the angels stand,
> High in the stainless eminence of air;
> The next, they were not; — to their Fatherland
> Translated unaware!"

THE MATTERHORN.

On my last evening at Zermatt, I lingered in the deepening twilight to say farewell to this unrivaled peak. At first its clear-cut silhouette stood forth against the sky, unutterably grand, while darkness shrouded its giant form. So overwhelming appeared its tapering height, that I no longer wondered at the belief of the peasants that the gate of Paradise was situated on its summit; because it seemed but a step thence to Heaven.

At last there came a change, for which I had been waiting with impatience. In the blue vault of heaven the full-orbed moon came forth to sheathe the Matterhorn in silver. In that refulgent light its icy edges looked like crystal ropes; and

THE BERNESE OBERLAND.

its sharp, glistening rocks resembled silver steps leading to the stupendous pinnacle above. Never, this side the shore of Eternity, do I expect to see a vision so sublime as that of moonlight on the Matterhorn. For from the gleaming parapets of this Alpine pyramid, not "forty centuries," but forty thousand ages look down on us as frivolous pygmies of a day. Yes, as I gazed on this illumined obelisk, rising from out its glittering sea of ice, to where — four thousand feet above — the moving stars flashed round its summit like resplendent gems, it seemed a fitting emblem of creative majesty — the scepter of Almighty God.

A SWISS HERO.

ATHENS

Athens

A NATION'S influence is not dependent on its size. Its glory is not measured by square miles. Greece is the smallest of all European countries, being not larger than the State of Massachusetts. Yet, in the light of what a few Athenians accomplished in the days of Phidias, China's four hundred millions seem like shadows cast by moving clouds. China compared to Athens! The enlightened world could better lose the entire continent of Asia from its history than that little area. Better fifty years of Athens than a cycle of Cathay. In the historic catalogue of earth's great cities Athens stands alone. The debt which civilization owes her is incalculable. For centuries Athens was the school of Rome, and through Rome's conquests she became the teacher of the world. If most of her art treasures had not been torn from her, first

ATHENE.

to embellish Rome, and subsequently to enrich the various museums of the world, Athens would now be visited by thousands instead of hundreds. But even in her desolation Athens repays a pilgrimage. Were absolutely nothing

of her glory left, it would still remain a privilege merely to
stand amid the scenes where human intellect reached a height
which our material progress has not equaled. They err who
say that Greece is dead. She cannot die. The Language of
Demosthenes is still extant. Not only are its accents heard
within the shadow of the Parthenon; it is so interwoven with
our own, that we unconsciously make use of its old words, as
one walks on a pavement of mosaic, unmindful whence its
pieces came. The Greek Religion lives in every statue of
the gods, in every classical allusion, in every myth which poets
weave into the garland of their song. What could a sculptor
do without the gods and heroes of old Greek mythology?
Hellenic Architecture lives in every reproduction of Doric
column or Corinthian capital. The Art of the Acropolis

remains the
standard for all
time. The His-
tory of Greece

OLD AND NEW.

still gives to us as
models of heroic patri-
otism, Thermopylæ and Marathon. Even
her ideas live,—the thoughts of Phidias in marble; of Plato in
philosophy; of Socrates in morals; of Euripides and Sophocles in tragedy.

What, then, if it be true that Greece has greatly changed
in twenty centuries? The influence of ancient Greece comes

VIEW OF MARS HILL FROM THE ACROPOLIS.

down the ages to us like the light from a fixed star. The
star itself may have gone out in darkness years ago; but
waves of brilliancy which left it previous to its destruction
are traveling toward us still, and fall in silvery pulsations on
our earth to-day. The best way to approach the shores of
Greece is over
the classic Medi-
terranean and
Ægean seas.
Around these
oceans gather
more thrilling
and inspiring as-
sociations than

THROUGH GRECIAN WATERS.

cluster about any others on the globe. Upon no equal area
of the earth's surface have so many mighty events happened or
deeds been enacted as around these inland seas. Every keel
that now cleaves their waters traverses the scene of some
maritime struggle or adventure of ancient times, or glides by
shores forever hallowed to the scholar and historian by the
memories of the genius and grandeur that have passed away.
To sail on Grecian waters is to float through history. The
seas of other countries gleam with phosphorescence; hers
sparkle with the scintillations of a deathless fame. The very
islands they caress have been the cradles of fable, poesy and
history. From each has sprung a temple, a statue, a poem,
or at least a myth, which still exists to furnish joy and inspiration to the world.

It is with the liveliest anticipations of pleasure that one
who is inspired by these memories, arrives at the port of
Athens, which still retains its ancient title,—The Piræus. Its
appearance is not especially attractive, and yet I gazed upon
it with profound emotion. Still are its waves as blue as when
Athenian vessels rode at anchor here, or swept hence to the

island of Salamis to aid in the destruction of the Persian fleet and cause the mad flight of the terror-stricken Xerxes. Around them History and Poetry have woven an immortal charm, for in their limpid depths have been reflected the forms of almost every famous Greek and Roman of antiquity.

But the Piræus, after all, is merely a doorway to glories beyond. Hence one quickly leaves the steamer here, and hastens to the capital itself, six miles away. A train of street-cars, drawn by a steam-engine, was one of the first objects that confronted us in the streets of Athens, but even this reminder of the nineteenth century could not dispel the fasci-nation of antiquity. It all swept back upon me. The loco-motive and the tram-cars faded from my view, and in their place I saw again my school-room, with its rows of well-worn desks. Once more was felt the summer breeze, as it stole through the open window, and lured me from my lexicon to the fair fields. Xenophon's graphic prose and Homer's match-less verse at last seemed real to me; for over the shop-doors were the Greek characters that I had learned in boyhood, and

THE DISTANT CITADEL.

on the corners of the streets were words once utter-ed by the lips of Socrates.

Even before the tourist reach-es the outskirts of the city of Minerva, he plainly sees rising in bold relief against the sky, what was in ancient times the gem of Athens, the casket of the rarest architectural jewels in the world,— the temple-crowned Acropolis. It is a memorable moment when one first beholds it. No other citadel in the world has embraced

so much beauty and splendor within its walls. Not one has
witnessed such startling changes in the fortunes of its posses-
sors. Its history reaches back over a period of two thousand four hundred years. Wave after wave of war and conquest have beaten against it. It has been plundered by the
Persian, the Spartan, the Mace-
donian, the Roman, the
Venetian and the Turk.
Yet there is now a
modern city at its base,

astonishingly new
and fresh, compar-
ed with its historic
background. The
buildings of to-day
and those of two
thousand years ago

A WALK AROUND THE ACROPOLIS.

seem gazing at each other with surprise. Yet there is no hos-
tility between them. Despite her tattered robes of royalty,
Old Athens sits enthroned as the acknowledged sovereign.
New Athens kneels in reverence before her. For the modern
Greeks still cling with pride to the memories of Pericles and
Phidias, and sigh when they think of the glory that once
was theirs.

A walk around the Acropolis reveals the fact that it is a
natural mass of rock, built up in places by substantial
masonry. On three sides it is practically perpendicular.
Two thousand years ago its summit rose toward heaven, like

a magnificent altar consecrated to the gods. There, elevated in the sight of all, and overlooking the adoring city on the one side and the blue Ægean on the other, stood those incomparable specimens of architectural beauty, grace and majesty, which have made Athens immortal. Even now, although its temples are in ruins, the few remaining columns of the Parthenon

stand out in delicate relief against the sky, like strings of an abandoned harp, which even the most skilful hand can never wake again to melody.

THE PROPYLÆA.

In making the ascent of this historic eminence by the only avenue of approach, the traveler soon finds himself before the ruined entrance to the Acropolis,—the Propylæa. This was originally a majestic gateway of Pentelic marble, crown-

ing a marble staircase seventy feet in breadth, which led up
from the city to the brow of the Acropolis. Its cost was
two and a half millions of dollars. It was considered, in its
prime, equal, if not superior, to the Parthenon. Nor is this
strange, for this portal was a veritable gallery of art. Along
its steps were arranged those chiseled forms that almost
lived and breathed in their transcendent beauty,—the masterpieces of Praxiteles and Phidias, the mutilated fragments of
which we now cherish as our most perfect models of the
beautiful.

Yet there was nothing effeminate in this magnificence.
Solidity and splendor here went hand in hand. When the
Propylæa was finished, under Pericles, more than four centuries
were still to pass before the birth of Christ; yet so much strength
was here combined with beauty, that, if no human hands had
striven to deface it, its splendid shafts would, no doubt,
still be perfect. The columns that remain appear to stand
like sentinels,   guarding their
illustrious   past. It

THE SUMMIT OF THE ACROPOLIS.

thrills one to reflect that these identical pillars have cast their shadows on the forms of Phidias, Pericles, Demosthenes, and indeed every Greek whose name has been preserved in history.

When I passed on beyond the Propylæa, and gained a broader view of the Acropolis, I looked around me with astonishment. The whole plateau is literally covered with headless statues, fallen columns and disjointed capitals. Some of them bear unfinished

THE PARTHENON,
EXTERIOR AND INTERIOR.

sentences, as though these blocks would speak, if they were properly restored. Their power of speech, however, has been forever paralyzed by the destructive blows they have received. This rugged rock is nevertheless an illustrated volume of Greek history bound in stone. Its letters are disfigured, its binding is defaced, but the old volume is still legible; and it assures us that this tiny platform, scarcely one thousand feet in length and four hundred in breadth, is richer in some respects than any other portion of the globe, for in the golden crucible of memory,

THE ACROPOLIS.

Art, History and Poetry transmute each particle of its sacred dust into a precious stone.

It is, however, to the highest point of the plateau that the tourist's gaze turns with keenest interest, for there stood what was formerly the crown of the Acropolis, the architectural glory of the world,—The Parthenon.

No photographic view can do it justice. Pictures invariably represent its marble columns as dark and dingy, like the sooty architecture of London. But such is not the case. The discolorations are so slight as hardly to be blemishes. The general appearance of the edifice is one of snowy whiteness, softly defined against the clear,

A PORTION OF THE FRIEZE.

blue sky, and I have seen its columns in the glow of sunset gleam like shafts of gold. But on approaching it more closely, one sees that nothing can conceal the ravages of time and man. Yet, only two hundred years ago it stood comparatively unchanged in its unrivaled beauty. The Turks were then the masters of this classic land. They showed their appreciation of the Parthenon by using it as a powder-magazine! In 1687 an army of Venetians recklessly bombarded Athens, and one of their shells exploded in this shrine. Instantly, with a wild roar, as though Nature herself shrieked at the sacrilege, the Parthenon was ruined. Columns on either side were blown to atoms, the front was severed from the rear,

and the entire hill was strewn with marble fragments, mute
witnesses of countless forms of beauty lost to us forever.

One of these fragments is a portion of the frieze that once
surrounded the entire edifice like a long garland of rare beauty.
How careful were the old Greek artists of their reputation;
how conscientious in their art! The figures in this frieze
were fifty feet above the ground, where small defects would

FRONT VIEW OF THE PARTHENON.

never have been noticed, yet every part of each was finished
with the utmost care. While they remained there for two
thousand years, this trait of old Greek character was unper-
ceived; but, with their downfall and removal, the sculptor's
grand fidelity to truth was brought to light,—as death sometimes reveals the noble qualities which we in life, alas! have
not observed.

Enough of the Parthenon remains to show the literal perfection of its masonry. It has, for example, in its steps,
walls, and columns, curves so minute as to be hardly visible,
yet true to the one-hundredth part of an inch. They

show alike the splendid genius of the architect and the wonderful skill of the workmen.   For all the curves are mathe-
matical.   The reasons for them can be demonstrated like a
problem in geometry.   Once fifty life-size statues stood upon
its pediments.   Around it ran a sculptured frieze, five hundred and twenty feet in length, carved mainly by the hand of
Phidias; while the especial treasure of the temple was the
famous statue of Athene Parthenos, made of ivory and gold.
The value of the precious metal used in this one figure was
seven hundred and fifty thousand dollars.

It is a marvel that any fragments can be gathered on the top
of the Acrop-
olis, after the
persistent spoli-
ation which
Greece has un-
dergone for more
than eighteen
centuries. From
the one city of

FRAGMENTS.

Delphi alone Nero is said to have carried off to Rome
five hundred bronze statues.   How many beautiful works
in marble, gold and ivory he removed, we cannot tell.
And when the Roman conqueror, Æmilius Paulus, was borne
in triumph up the Appian Way, exhibiting the spoils of conquered Greece, there preceded him two hundred and fifty
wagons filled with the rarest pictures and statues of Greek
artists, after which came three thousand men, each bearing
some gold or silver ornament taken from Hellenic cities. Yet
this was merely the beginning of the plundering, which practically ended only fifty years ago, when Lord Elgin carried
off to London over two hundred and fifty feet of the beautifully sculptured frieze of the Parthenon. Opinions differ
in regard to the propriety of this act on the part of Lord

Elgin. Defenders of his conduct urge that, had this not been done, these works of art would have been ruined by the Turks. Others maintain that they would have remained intact, and point to some of the comparatively uninjured decorations of the shrines of the Acropolis, such as the Caryatides of the Erectheum, which have at least never been injured by the Turks, though one of them was removed to

SOME OF THE SPOILS.

England by Lord Elgin. At all events, it would be a noble and graceful act on the part of England particularly, and of many other countries also, to restore some of her lost art-treasures to Greece,—now that she has risen again to the rank of a well-governed and progressive nation. It is sad indeed to see in Athens only plaster casts of the incomparable works of her old sculptors, the originals of which enrich so many European capitals.

One of the most beautiful of the ruined shrines of the Acropolis is the "Temple of Wingless Victory;" so-called because the statue of the goddess was represented without wings, in the fond hope that Victory would never fly away from the Athenian capital. Most of the beautiful statues which adorned this building were carried off to the British Museum seventy years ago, and some were ruined in the process of removal. One exquisite portion of the frieze, which had for twenty centuries stood forth resplendent over the historic city, was carelessly dropped and broken into atoms. A Greek who was standing near, watching this shameful devastation, brushed away a tear, and with a sob exclaimed pathetically: " Telos! " (That is the end of it!) and turned away.

No one has condemned the plunder of the Acropolis more trenchantly than Byron, in the lines:

> " Cold is the heart, fair Greece! that looks on thee,
>   Nor feels as lovers o'er the dust they loved ;
>   Dull is the eye that will not weep to see
>   Thy walls defaced, thy mouldering shrines removed
>   By British hands, which it had best behooved
>   To guard those relics ne'er to be restored.
>   Curst be the hour when from their isle they roved,
>   And once again thy hapless bosom gored,
>   And snatch'd thy shrinking Gods to northern climes abhorr'd!"

Before the mental vision of the traveler, who muses thus upon the crest of the Acropolis, there naturally rises the form of the goddess Athene (or, as the Romans called her, Minerva), who gave the name Athens to the city which she specially protected. Who can forget how this old classic citadel, within whose shrines this goddess was adored, remained for many centuries, even in its ruin, a beacon light of

THE CARYATIDES OF THE ERECTHEUM.

history?   Its radiance pierced even the darkness of the Middle Ages, when, over-run by conquerors, pillaged by barbarians, assailed by fanatics, the world of art lay buried beneath the rubbish of brutality and ignorance.   Under the blows of the iconoclasts, the pulse of artistic life had almost ceased to beat. But, though the fire of genius seemed extinct, there was still vitality in its dying embers. The light which came from the Acropolis gave its illumination to the Renaissance. Without an Athens there had been no Florence; without a Phidias no Michael Angelo.

PORTAL OF THE ERECTHEUM.

Almost as interesting as a visit to the summit of the Acropolis is a walk around its base. A part of it is lined with ruins, many of them being demolished theatres.   Upon the hill the drama of the gods went on: below it were performed the tragedy and comedy of man.   One of these theatres, called the Odeon, was of Roman origin, built by the conquerors of Greece when they were masters of the world. Its rows of massive arches, climbing one above another up the cliff, remind us of the Colosseum.   Above them was the classic Parthenon, which Phidias had built five hundred years

before. This theatre could accommodate eight thousand people, and
doubtless was magnificent and imposing; but amid such surroundings
it must have seemed to the Athenians like an interloper and intruder,
— a gilded fetter on a lovely slave.

Vastly more interesting, however,
than the Odeon is the edifice which
adjoins it,— the ancient theater of
Bacchus,— built by the Greeks two
thousand four hundred years ago. It
was excavated from the side of the
Acropolis, just below the Parthenon.
Its rows of seats were partly sculptured from the solid rock and partly
built up of Pen-
telic marble,
and thirty

ATHENE.

thousand people could be seated
here. Its form was a perfect amphitheatre, a model for all others
in the world. How grand was its
simplicity! Its light was furnished by the sun. God was the
painter of its drop-curtain, which
was the sunset sky; the scenery
was that of mountains and the
sea; its only roof was the blue
dome of heaven.

A portion of the front of the
old stage is still intact. If the
old Greeks had needed footlights,
they would have placed them

MERCURY.

on this marble parapet. It sends the
blood in a swift current to the heart to
think that all its kneeling or support-
ing statues have listened to the plays
of Aristophanes or Sophocles, and
have beheld innumerable audiences oc-
cupying the marble seats which still
confront them. Alas! What have they
not beheld here since those glorious
days! In this, the earliest home of
tragedy, how many tragedies have
been enacted! Directly opposite this

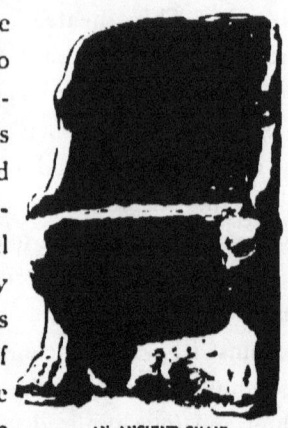

AN ANCIENT CHAIR.

parapet is one of the ancient marble seats. It was occupied
by an Athenian magistrate more than two thousand years ago.
His name is still inscribed upon it, — perfectly legible, and
defiant of the touch of Time. Standing in this amphitheatre,
one realizes as never before, how, in an epoch of great intel-

lectual activity, genius does
not confine itself to one
particular line. Whether it
be the age of Pericles, the

THE ODEON.

Renaissance, the era of Elizabeth, or the magnificent century of the Moors, a wave of mental energy rolls over an entire nation.   Thus here, at Athens, it was not only sculpture that attained such excellence, but painting; not only painting but architecture; not only architecture but oratory; not only oratory but philosophy; and in addition to all these, this wonderful city gave mankind the drama, so perfect at the start that even the modern world, with all its literary culture and experience, regards the old Greek dramatists as its masters. Filled with such thoughts, one seems to see, while lingering here, the form of Sopho-

INTERIOR OF THE ODEON.

cles, the greatest of Greek tragic poets.   For more than two thousand three hundred years his plays have been admired as almost perfect models of dramatic composition.   There is hardly a university in the world that has not one of his magnificent tragedies in its curriculum of study.   His play of "Œdipus the King," which is so well interpreted by the French actor, Mounet Sully, is still a masterpiece of strength

SOPHOCLES.

and majesty; and all his other plays, together with those of Æschylus, Euripides, and Aristophanes, have in their lofty sentiments never been surpassed, unless, indeed, by those of Shakespeare. Inspired by the memory of these Hellenic heroes, I approached (still almost in the shadow of the Acropolis) a rocky ledge, known as the "Platform of Demosthenes." Rough and unshapely though it be, in view of all that has transpired on its summit it is of greater value to the world than if the entire hill were paved with gold and studded with the rarest gems. From this rock the orators of Athens spoke to the assembled people. Before it then was the Athenian market-place,—the forum of the city. The site is perfectly identified, and one can look upon the very spot from which Demosthenes delivered his orations, still unsurpassed in ancient or in modern times even by those of Cicero and Burke.

THE THEATRE OF BACCHUS.

Truly, as Byron says, in Athens

" Where'er we tread 'tis haunted holy ground,
No earth of thine is lost in vulgar mould,
But one vast realm of wonder spreads around,
And all the Muse's tales seem truly told,
Till the sense aches with gazing to behold
The scenes our earliest dreams have dwelt upon."

Leaving this noble relic of the past, I presently stood before a solitary gate, known as " The Arch of Hadrian." It was, in fact, erected here by that Roman emperor in the second century after Christ, when Greece was but a province of the Cæsars. In Italy this would seem to us of great antiquity; but amid objects such as I had just beheld, it appeared com-

THE FRONT OF THE STAGE.

paratively modern. On one side of this portal is the inscription, " This is Athens, the old City of Theseus." On the other are the words, " This is the new City of Hadrian, not that of Theseus." In fact this gateway was a barrier, yet a connecting link, between the Grecian and the Roman Athens,—the cities of the conquered and the conqueror.

Looking through this historic arch, I saw a group of stately columns in the distance. They are the only relics that remain of the great Temple of Olympian Jove. Even the writers of antiquity, familiar though they were with splendid structures,

speak of that
shrine as being
awe-inspiring in
its grandeur.
With the ex-
ception of the
Temple of
Diana at Ephe-
sus, it was the
largest Grecian
temple ever
built. There
were, original-

PLATFORM OF DEMOSTHENES.

ly, at least one hundred and twenty-six of these Corinthian columns. They formed almost a marble forest. Within it was a veritable maze of statues, including one of Jupiter, which was world-renowned; but these, as well as nearly all the columns, have long since been abstracted or destroyed.

These marble giants do not form a single group. Two of them stand apart, like sentries stationed to give warning of the fresh approach of the despoiler. Between them one column lies prostrate; a sad reminder of the fate that has overtaken so many of its brethren. However, unlike most other ruins in the world, this was not caused by the maliciousness of man. On the night of the 26th of October, 1852, a heavy rainstorm under-mined the soil at its base, and the huge column, overcome

at last, fell its full length of sixty feet upon the sand.   It
is interesting to observe how evenly its massive sections still
rest upon the ground, like bricks set up in rows to push each
other over in their fall.

It is said that the prostrate column could be restored, but
perhaps it is more eloquent as it lies.   The shaft above it,
with its beautiful Corinthian capital, presents a striking contrast.   One seems proudly to say, " See
what this noble temple was!" the other
to murmur pathetically, " See what it
is to-day!"

Continuing my way still farther
round the base of the Acropolis, I
presently perceived a low-browed hill,
partially covered with a rocky ledge.
It was the ancient Areopagus, or Hill
of Mars.   Here the Supreme Court of

TEMPLE OF OLYMPIAN JOVE.

THE ARCH OF HADRIAN.

Athens held its sessions. Such was the simple grandeur of the old Athenians that the only covering of this court-room was the canopy of heaven. For the immortal gods no temple could be too magnificent; but for the serious business of deciding life and death the Greeks would have no sumptuous decoration. The sessions of the court were always held at night, so that no face or gesture could exert the slightest influence. It must have been a scene of wonderful solemnity, for here accusers and accused stood, as it were, between their venerable judges and the gods, while in the dome of night a cloud of glittering witnesses looked down upon them from illimitable space.

A flight of sixteen rough-hewn steps leads to the summit, where

THE SENTINELS.

the judges sat. They are the ancient steps. By them
St. Paul ascended to address the Athenian audience which
gathered before him. Above him, as he spoke, rose the

MARS HILL.

whole glory of
the Acropolis,
with its mag-
nificent temples
and bewilder-
ing array of
statues. And
yet this stran-
ger dared to
utter the im-
pressive words,
"God dwelleth not in temples made with hands." This in
the shadow of the Parthenon! "We ought not to think
that the Godhead is like unto gold or silver, or stone graven
by art and man's device." This in the presence of the
works of Phidias!

When we remember how the Acropolis must then have
looked, we cannot wonder that the Athenians who heard
these words spoken
within its shadow
smiled, and ironi-
cally answered,
"We will hear thee
again of this mat-
ter!" Well, Athens
has heard him
again, and so has the
entire world. Paul

IN THE TIME OF PAUL.

discoursed here for possibly an hour, but what he said has
ever since been echoing down the ages. None knew him then;
but in a few short years, to the church founded by him in the

Greek town of Corinth, he wrote his two epistles to the Corinthians, which may be read in every language of the civilized world; and now there is hardly a city in all Christendom that has not a cathedral or church bearing the great Apostle's name.

Not far from this historic spot is another ledge of great antiquity. Here dungeons have been excavated in the solid rock, one of them being called the "Prison of Socrates."

PRISON OF SOCRATES.

Opinions differ as to its authenticity; just as men still dispute about the exact locality where Jesus hung upon the Cross. But of the general situation in each case there is no doubt. In Athens, as in Jerusalem, one stands in close proximity to where the purest souls this earth has ever known were put to death by those who hated them; and somewhere on this hill, four hundred years before the scene of Calvary, Socrates drank the poisoned cup forced upon him by his enemies, and in that draught found immortality.

The lineaments of Christ's face are not surely known to us, but those of Socrates have been preserved in marble. His was a plain and homely visage. The playwright, Aristophanes, caricatured him on the stage, and moved the audience to shouts of laughter; but, with the exception of the Nazarene, no man ever spoke like Socrates. He was a natural teacher of men. He walked daily among the temples or in the market-place, talking with every one who cared to listen to him. His method was unique. It was, by asking searching questions, to force men to think,— to know themselves. If he could make an astonished man give utterance to an original thought, he was contented for that day. He had sown the seed; it would bear fruit. He had no notes, nor did he ever write a line; yet his incomparable thoughts, expressed in purest speech, were faithfully recorded by his pupils, Xenophon and Plato, and will be treasured to the end of time.

SOCRATES.

Another memorial of Athens which well repays a visit is the Temple of Theseus,— that legendary hero of old Greece, half-man, half-god, whose exploits glimmer through the dawn of history, much as a mountain partially reveals itself through morning mists. Fortune has treated this old temple kindly. There is hardly an ancient structure extant that has so perfectly resisted the disintegrating touch of time or the destroying hand of man. For the

Theseum was built nearly five hundred years before the birth of Christ, in commemoration of the glorious battle of Marathon, where Theseus was believed to have appeared to aid the Greeks in driving from their shores the invading Persians.

When in 1824 Lord Byron died upon Greek soil, striving to free the Hellenic nation from the Turkish yoke, the Athenians wished his body to be buried in this temple. No wonder

TEMPLE OF THESEUS.

they were grateful to him, for the action of that ardent admirer of the Greeks in hastening to their land to consecrate his life and fortune to the cause of liberty, was not, as some have thought, unpractical and sentimental. Byron, unlike many other poets, was no mere dreamer. He could, when he desired, descend from Poesy's empyrean to the practical realities of life; and during his short stay in Greece, whether he was securing loans, conciliating angry chiefs, or giving counsel to the government, he showed the tact and firmness of an able statesman.

As if, then, this classic temple were a Greek sarcophagus, within which was enshrined the form of the immortal dead,

I seemed to see among its marble columns that noble statue representing Byron at Missolonghi, the little town where, with such fatal haste, his life was sacrificed. It would be difficult to imagine anything more distressing than Byron's last illness. He was in a wretched, malarial district, utterly devoid of comforts. No woman's hand was there to smooth his brow or give to him the thousand little comforts which only woman's tender thoughtfulness can understand. Convinced at last by the distress of his servants that his death was

BYRON AT MISSOLONGHI.

near, he called his faithful valet, Fletcher, to his side, and spoke with great earnestness, but very indistinctly, for nearly twenty minutes. Finally he said, with relief, " Now I have told you all."

" My lord," replied Fletcher, " I have not understood a word you have been saying."

" Not understood me?" exclaimed Lord Byron, with a look of the utmost distress. " What a pity! for it is too late; all is over!"

" I hope not," answered Fletcher, " but the Lord's will be done."

" Yes, not mine," said the poet; and soon after murmured, " Now I shall go to sleep." These were the last

A RUINED CAPITAL.

words of Byron, for, with a weary sigh, he then sank into that peaceful slumber in which his spirit gradually loosed its hold on earth, and drifted outward into the Unknown.

The more modern part of Athens recalls happier recollections of Byron. When he came here in his youth, he not only

wrote those magnificent stanzas in "Childe Harold," which are among the choicest treasures of our English tongue, but also composed that graceful poem, " Maid of Athens," each verse of which ends with Greek words that signify, " My Life, I love thee!" It was addressed to the eldest daughter of the Greek lady in whose house he lodged. Little did that fair Athenian girl imagine that his verses would

MAID OF ATHENS

make her known throughout the world. Yet so it was. No actual likeness of her can be given, but we may well believe that she, in some respects, resembled a typical Grecian maiden of to-day.

> " By those tresses unconfined,
> Woo'd by each Ægean wind;
> By those lids whose jetty fringe
> Kiss thy soft cheeks' blooming tinge;
> By those wild eyes like the roe,
> Ζώη μοῦ, σάς ἀγαπῶ.

> By that lip I long to taste;
> By that zone-encircled waist;
> By all the token-flowers that tell
> What words can never speak so well;
> By love's alternate joy and woe,
> Ζώη μοῦ, σάς ἀγαπῶ.

Maid of Athens! I am gone:
Think of me, sweet! when alone.
Though I fly to Istambol,
Athens holds my heart and soul:
Can I cease to love thee? No!
Ζώη μοῦ, σὰς ἀγαπῶ."

The tourist who visits Greece to-day finds much to admire in the modern city which ancient Athens wears now like a jewel on her withered breast. It is a bright, attractive place. When I revisited it a few years ago, it seemed to me by contrast with the Orient a miniature Paris. Yet this is all of very recent growth. Half a century ago the devastation wrought here by the Turks had left the city desolate. Hardly a house in the whole town was habitable. But now we find a city of one hundred and thirty thousand people, with handsome residences, public squares, clean streets, and several public buildings that would adorn any capital in the world.

One of the finest private residences in Athens is the home of the late Doctor Schliemann, the world-renowned explorer of the plain of Troy   and other sites of Greek antiq-   uity.   It

THE BYZANTINE CHURCH.

is constructed of pure Pentelic marble. Around its roof beautiful groups of statuary gleam white against the blue of the Athenian sky. Anywhere else this style of decoration would perhaps seem out of place; not so in Athens. It simply serves as a reminder of the fact that once the wealth of art here was so great that half the galleries of the world are filled to-day with the fragments of it that remain. So many statues once ex-

RESIDENCE OF DOCTOR SCHLIEMANN.

isted here, that an Athenian wit declared that it was easier to find a god in Athens than a man!

Perhaps the finest of the public build-ings in Athens is its Academy of Science. It is a noble struc-ture, composed

entirely of Pentelic marble and built in imitation of the classic style, with rows of grand Ionic columns, while in the pediment are sculptures resembling those with which the Greeks two thousand years ago adorned the shrines of the Acropolis. The lofty marble columns in the foreground are crowned with figures of Minerva and Apollo. Below them are the seated statues of Socrates and Plato. What more appropriate combination could be made than this: the wisdom of the gods above, the wisdom of humanity below, expressed by the greatest names which in religion and philosophy have given Athens an immortal fame? In the spring of 1896 modern Athens seemed suddenly to surpass the ancient

ATHENS FROM THE ODEON OF HEROD.

city in interest, through the revival of the Olympian games.
The mention of these famous contests suggests at once
the old Greek statue of the Disk-Thrower, whose arm
has been uplifted for the admiration of the world for
more than two thousand years. Although this national
festival of the Greeks had its origin nearly eight hundred
years before the birth of Christ, and though the last one

THE ACADEMY OF SCIENCE.

was celebrated fifteen hundred years ago, the games were
renewed in 1896 as the first of a series of international athletic
contests, which will hereafter take place every four years in
various portions of the world. The first was given, of course,
to Greece, the mother of athletics as she was of art. The
next will be seen at Paris in 1900, during the Exposition
there.

For the great occasion referred to, the old Greek Stadium
was partially re-excavated and furnished with hundreds of
new marble seats. This was done not alone at the expense of

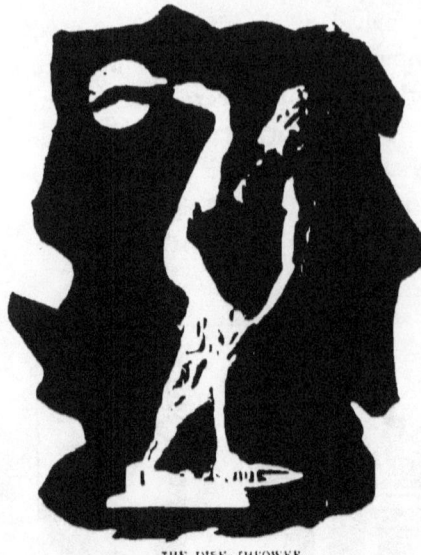

THE DISK-THROWER.

a few rich Athenians, but also through the generosity of wealthy Greeks in Alexandria, Smyrna, London, and Marseilles. The Stadium, as it now exists, can accommodate about sixty thousand people; and on the closing day of the recently revived festival, fully that number were assembled in it, while forty thousand more were grouped outside the walls or on the road between Athens and the battlefield of Marathon. Among the contesting athletes were several manly specimens of "Young America." In every way they did us honor. Those with whom we talked on the subject spoke in the highest terms of the courtesy and kindness shown them by every one in Athens, from king to peasant. Nor was this strange. It was due, first, to their own fine qualities; second, to the popularity which America enjoys in Greece, and third, to the fact that they themselves soon proved the heroes of the Stadium.

After each contest, the flag of the victorious country was displayed above the arena, and the American emblem was the first to go up. And it kept going up! The first three races were all

AN ATHLETE.

won by Americans. Then came the "long jump," which
Americans also gained. Then Garrett, of Princeton, beat
the Greeks themselves at their old classic sport of "throwing the disk." Even on the second day "Old Glory"
shook out its starry folds three times, till presently Denmark
gained a victory, and then England.

THE STADIUM.

It is hard to single out for special notice any one individual among these heroes; but no American gained more popularity on the historic race-course, than the man who for swift
running carried off so many prizes in Old Athens,—that lithe
citizen of the "Athens of America," Thomas Burke. Over
his speed and skill the Greeks were wildly enthusiastic.
Some of them showed him proofs of personal affection. One
asked him, through an interpreter, on what food he had been
trained. Burke, like a true Bostonian, replied, "Beans!"
After one of his brilliant victories, when the Americans

had gained in swift succession four first prizes, one old Athenian stood up in the Stadium, and raising his hands in mock despair, exclaimed: "O, why did Columbus ever discover that country!"

Finally, on the last day, there came a contest which the Greeks had been awaiting with alternating hope and fear. It

SOME OF THE AMERICAN ATHLETES.

was the long run from the battlefield of Marathon to Athens, — a distance of twenty-five miles.

Besides the Greeks, there entered for this race Americans, Australians, Frenchmen, Germans, and Hungarians. Secretly, however, almost every one of the spectators hoped that a Greek would win. History and sentiment alike seemed to demand that the coveted honor should be gained by a descendant of the men of Marathon, for this was the same road traversed by the historic Greek, who ran to announce to the Athenians the triumph of the Greeks over the Persians at Marathon, and as he entered the Arena, dropped dead, gasping the word, "Victory!"

Instinctively that scene rises before the reader's imagination, as it must have done before the minds of the thousands gathered on the course to witness the issue of the race. It was half-past four in the afternoon when a cannon-shot announced that the leading runner

THOMAS BURKE.

was in sight. Two or three minutes passed in breathless silence. No one moved or spoke. Suddenly, a far-off cry was heard, "It is a Greek — a Greek!" These words were taken up and ran the whole length of the Stadium as electricity leaps from point to point. A moment more, and a hundred thousand voices rent the air with cheers and acclamations. The king himself almost tore the visor from his cap, waving it frantically round his head; for, in truth, the victor *was a Greek*, — a young peasant named Loues, twenty-four

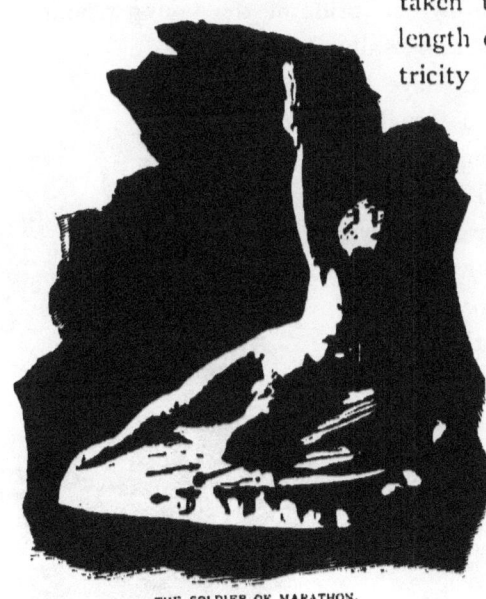

THE SOLDIER OF MARATHON.

LOUES.

years of age.   Before entering the contest, he had partaken of the sacrament and had invoked the aid of Heaven; and apparently the gods had come to his assistance, for he had made the run of twenty-five miles over a hard, rough country in *two hours and forty-five minutes!*   To show the feeling the victor entertained for the American athletes, it may be said that when Loues crossed the line, notwithstanding the tremendous excitement and enthusiasm that prevailed, he ran to Tom Burke, and, throwing his arms around him, kissed the American flag which the Bostonian was holding in his hand.

At the king's palace, Loues and the other competing athletes were entertained in royal style by the crowned head of the kingdom.   The joy and pride of the young peasant's father, as he saw him universally fêted and admired, is said to have been extremely beautiful and touching; for Loues was treated almost as a demigod by his delighted countrymen. The strangest gifts were showered upon him.   A café, for example, offered him *carte blanche* at its hospitable table for the rest of his life; a barber-shop promised him free shaves so long as he lived; and even a boot-black coveted the honor of polishing his shoes for an indefinite period, expecting nothing in return. Large sums of money also were

THE "LANTERN OF DEMOSTHENES."

offered him; but these, with the true spirit of the athlete, Loues declined. "The only reward I crave," he exclaimed, "is the wreath of laurel from Olympia, such as my ancestors received two thousand years ago. I am poor, but I ran, not for money, but for the glory of my native land."

The pleasantest route in taking leave of the Hellenic kingdom is to embark upon a steamer and sail through the Grecian Archipelago. It is the same route taken by the old Greek colonists when they went forth to civilize the world,— the same path followed by the Trojan exiles when they sailed to Italy to build upon her seven hills the walls of Rome. To coast along the shores of the Ægean, after a tour in Athens, is one of the most exquisite enjoyments this life can give. To the student of history in particular, the scene recalls events so glorious that he is lost in admiration, not only of the marvelous country as a whole, but of what the ancient Greeks accomplished for humanity. In what department did they not excel?

VENUS OF MELOS.

Is it their sculpture that we question? At once the incomparable Venus of Melos makes reply; that statue found (alas! in partial ruin) on one of the islands that are scattered broadcast on this classic sea, like disentangled pearls, and hence a fitting emblem of those treasures of antiquity cast on the shores of time after a long-continued and disastrous storm.

Is it their language? It was the most perfect and elastic tongue in which men's lips have ever fashioned speech. It seems more than chance that caused it, at the birth of Christ, to be the leading literary language of the world, that it might thus receive, embody, and perpetuate the truths of the New Testament. Even now we turn to that old tongue to find exact expression for our terms of science, and in it we name all our new inventions such as heliotypes and photographs, the telegraph and the telephone.

HOMER.

Is it poetry? At once there seems to rise before us from these waters, which encircled him at birth and death, the face of Homer,— the father of poetry. To whom has he not been a joy and inspiration? Virgil was but the pupil and imitator of Homer. And the Iliad and Odyssey are still such storehouses of eloquence and beauty, that such statesmen as Gladstone and the Earl of Derby have sharpened their keen intellects in making their translations.

Is it philosophy? "Out of Plato," says Emerson, "come all things that are still written and debated among men of thought."

The lesson, then, which Athens teaches us is this: not to regard past men, past deeds, and ruined shrines as dead and useless limbs upon the Tree of Time. The Past has made the Present, just as the Present is now fashioning Futurity. Moreover, since one lofty sentiment begets another; one valiant deed inspires a second; and one sublime achievement is a

PLATO.

stepping-stone to loftier heights; what portion of our earth can give to us more inspiration than Athens,—birthplace of the earliest masterpieces of the human race, the mother of imperishable memories, and of an art that conquers time.

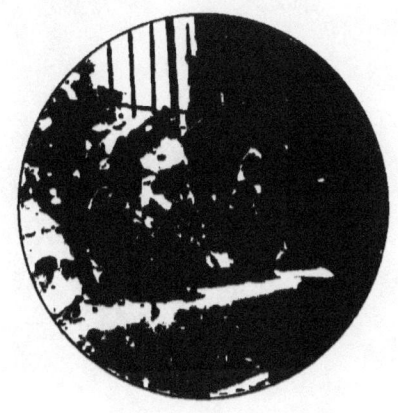

VENICE

VENICE

VENICE is still victorious over Time. Despite her age, the City of the Sea is fascinating still. She has successfully defied a dozen centuries; she may perhaps defy as many more. All other cities in the world resemble one another. Venice remains unique. She is the City of Romance—the only place on earth to-day where Poetry conquers Prose. The marriage of the Adriatic and its bride has never been dissolved. She is to-day, as she has been for fourteen hundred years, a capital whose streets are water and whose vehicles are boats. She is an incomparable illustration of the poetical and the picturesque; and, were she nothing else, would still attract the world. But she is infinitely more. The hands of Titian and Tintoretto have embellished her.

STATUE OF VICTOR EMANUEL.

She wears upon her breast some architectural jewels unsurpassed in Italy. And, finally, the splendor of her history enfolds her like the glory of her golden sunsets, and she emerges

from the waves of Time, that have repeatedly endeavored to
engulf her, as do her marble palaces from the encircling sea.

The charm of Venice begins even at what is usually the
most prosaic of places—a railway station. For, to a city
where there are no living horses, the iron horse at least has made
its way; and by a bridge, two miles in length, Venice is now

THE RAILWAY STATION.

connected with the outer world by rail. A quick, delicious
feeling of surprise comes over one to see awaiting him in the
place of carriages a multitude of boats. The pleasing sense
of novelty (so rare now in the world) appeals to us at once,
and, with the joyful consciousness of entering on a long-
anticipated pleasure, we seat ourselves within a gondola, and
noiselessly and swiftly glide out into the unknown.

The first surprise awaiting almost every visitor to Venice
is that of seeing all its buildings rise directly from the sea.
He knows, of course, that Venice rests upon a hundred islands,

THE BAY OF VENICE.

linked by four hundred and fifty bridges. Hence, he expects
to see between the houses and the liquid streets some fringe
of earth, some terrace or embankment. But no:—the stately
mansions emerge from the ocean like a huge sea-wall, and,
when the surface of the water is disturbed
by a light breeze or passing boat,
it overflows their marble
steps as softly as the
ultimate ripple of
the surf spreads its
white foam along
the beach. As,
then, our gondolier

A LIQUID LABYRINTH.

takes us farther through this
liquid labyrinth, we naturally
ask in astonishment, "What
was the origin of this mysterious city? How came it
to be founded thus within the
sea?" The wonder is easily
explained. In the fifth cen-

"LIKE A HUGE SEA-WALL."

tury after Christ, when the old Roman empire had well-nigh
perished under the deadly inroads of barbarians, another
devastating army entered Italy, led by a man who was
regarded as the "scourge of God." This man was Attila.
Such was the ruin always left behind him, that he could
boast with truth that the grass grew not where his horse had

trod.   A few men seeking to escape this vandal, fled to a
group of uninhabited islands in the Adriatic.   Exiled from
land, they cast themselves in desperation on the sea.

But no one can behold this ocean-city without perceiving that those exiles were rewarded for their courage.   The

THE OCEAN CITY.

sea became their mother, — their divinity.   She sheltered
them with her encircling waves.   She nourished them from
her abundant life.   She forced them to build boats in which
to transport merchandise from land to land.   And they, obey-
ing her, grew from a feeble colony of refugees to be a power-
ful republic, and made their city a nucleus of vast wealth and
commerce,—a swinging door between the Orient and Occi-
dent, through which there ebbed and flowed for centuries a

tide of golden
wealth, of which
her glorious sun-
sets seemed but
the reflection.

Who can for-
get his first
glimpse of the
Grand Canal?
Seen at a favor-
able hour, the
famous thorough-
fare delights the
senses as it thrills
the heart. For

THE GRAND CANAL.

two miles it winds through the city in such graceful lines
that every section of its course reveals a stately curve. Upon
this beautiful expanse the sun of Venice, like a cunning
necromancer, displays most marvelous effects of light and
shade, transforming it at different hours of the day into
an avenue of lapis-lazuli, or emerald, or gold,—an eloquent
reminder of the
time when Venice
was a paradise of
pleasure, when life
upon its liquid
streets was a per-
petual pageant,
and this incom-
parable avenue its
splendid promen-
ade. Its curving
banks are lined
with palaces.

VENETIAN PALACES.

They seem to be standing hand in hand, saluting one another gravely, as though both shores were executing here the movements of some courtly dance. These were originally the homes of men whose names were written in that record of Venetian nobility, called "The Book of Gold." Once they were marvels of magnificence; and viewed in the sunset light, or by the moon, they are so still. Under that enchanting spell their

A MARINE PORTE COCHÈRE.

massive columns, marble balconies, and elegantly sculptured arches, seem as imposing as when the Adriatic's Bride was still a queen and wore her robes of purple and of gold.

To build such structures on the shifting sands was a stupendous undertaking; and what we cannot see of these Venetian palaces has cost much more than that which rises now above the waves. From every door broad marble steps descend to the canal, and tall posts, painted with the colors of the family, serve as a mooring place for gondolas, a kind of marine *porte cochère*. Each of these structures has its legend,—poetic, tragic or artistic; and these our gondolier

BROWNING PALACE.

successively murmurs to us in his soft Venetian dialect as we glide along the glittering highway.

Thus, in the Palazzo Vendramini, the composer Wagner died in 1883. Not far from this stately mansion is the home of Desdemona. Within another of these palaces the old Doge Foscari died of a broken heart at the ill-treatment of his countrymen. In one lived Byron; in another Robert Browning; in a third George Sand; a fourth was once the home of Titian.

But now our winding course reveals to us, suspended over this noble thoroughfare, a structure which we recognize at once—"The Bridge of the Rialto." For centuries this was

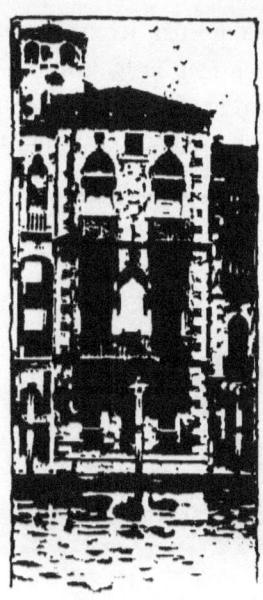

HOME OF DESDEMONA

the only bridge that crossed the Grand Canal. An ugly one of iron has been constructed near the railway station; but this Rialto remains a relic of Venice in her glory, for its huge

IN THE DAYS OF SHYLOCK.

arch is entirely of marble, and has a length of over a hundred and fifty feet. Its cost exceeded half a million dollars; and the foundations, which for three hundred and twenty years have faithfully supported it, are twelve thousand trunks of elm trees, each ten feet in length. To-day, little shops are built along the bridge, leaving a passageway between them in the centre and one without on either side.

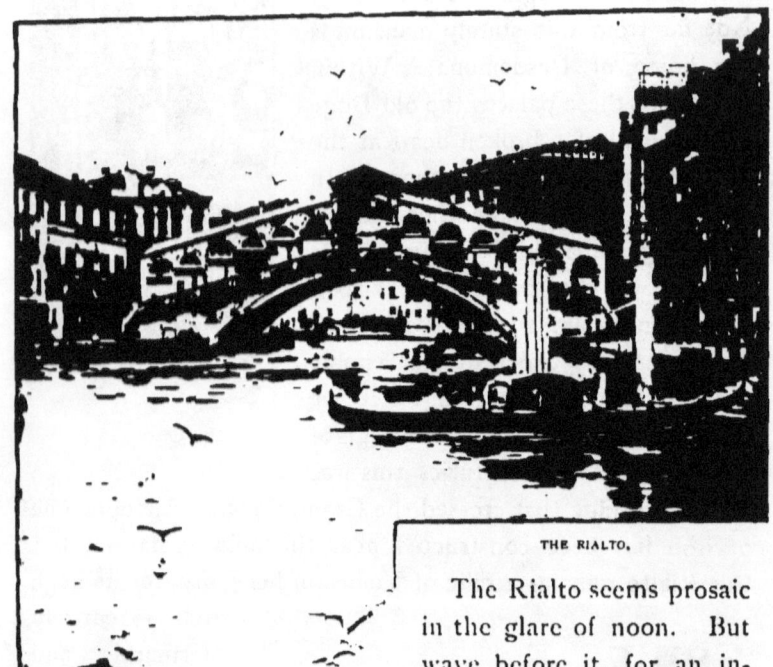

THE RIALTO.

The Rialto seems prosaic in the glare of noon. But wave before it, for an instant, the magic wands of fancy and historical association, and we can picture to ourselves how it must have looked when on this Rivo-Alto, or "High Bank," which gives the bridge its name, Venetian ladies saw outspread before them the treasures of the Orient; when at this point the laws of the Republic were proclaimed; when merchants congregated here as to a vast Exchange; and when, on this same bridge, the forms of Shylock and Othello may

have stood out in sharp relief against the sky; when, in a
word, Venice, like Venus, had been born of the blue sea,
possessing all the fascinating languor of the East, and yet
belonging to the restless West.   But to ac-
quire that mental state in   which
these visions of Vene-
tian splendor will re-
cur to one, certain
conditions are

THE CITY OF SILENCE.

essential for the tourist: first, he must choose the moon for
his companion; and, second, he must manage to arrive in
the City of the Sea by night. Venice, though beautiful,
shows marks of age. The glare of day is far too strong for

VENICE BY MOONLIGHT.

her pathetically fair, but wrinkled, face. Pay her the compliment to see her at her best. In Venice make your nights and days exchange places. Sleep through the morning hours, and spend the afternoons reading books that tell of old Venetian glory. Then, when the daylight wanes, and the moon turns these streets into paths of shimmering gold, go forth to woo *Venezia*, and she will give you of her best.

The form of the Grand Canal is that of a huge letter "S." Whenever it is looked upon from an elevation, this "S" is suggestive of the Italian word *Silenzio*, for Venice is pre-eminently the City of Silence. No roar of wheels disturbs one here; no strident gongs; no tramp of horses'

ON THE GRAND CANAL.

THE RIALTO.

feet. Reclining on the cushions of a gondola, one floats in absolute tranquillity upon a noiseless sea.

To go to another city after Venice is like removing from one's ears the fingers which for a little time had closed them to all sounds. No place is better for a weary brain-worker than Venice. His nerves relax in its restful stillness. The hand of Nature gently lifts the veil from his hot, wearied eyes; and he perceives at last that when a comfortable livelihood has been secured, to keep on toiling feverishly in the modern

A FAMILIAR SCENE.

world, beneath a pall of soot and in the midst of noisy, heartless crowds, is not to live: it is merely preparing to die.

Upon a moonlit night these liquid corridors present a scene too beautiful for words. It is the Venice of one's dreams. According to the light or shade, we glide through alternating paths of glory and of gloom. All the defects which day reveals are, by moonlight, totally concealed or softened into indistinctness, like features hidden by a silvery veil. Here and there some lights are gleaming through the casements; but, as a rule, the city seems to sleep.

Occasionally, it may be, a boat full of musicians will appear, and, to the passionate throbbing of the harp or guitar, a score of voices chant the songs of Italy. Meanwhile, a dozen gondolas, with listening occupants, float in the shadows of the marble palaces. These, when the music ceases, approach the expectant singers, and silver coins fall into outstretched hands, which glisten phantom-like for a moment in the moonlight. Then each gondola, with swan-like grace, in silence disappears, leaving behind it a long furrow like a chain of gold.

THE HEART OF VENICE.

When the visitor to Venice prepares to leave for a time his gondola, there is no need to say where he will land. There is one little area more important than all others, which every tourist longs to see and explore. It is a perfectly familiar scene, yet I have often noticed, with a thrill of sympathy, a tremor in the voice of the enthusiastic traveler who sees it for the first time, as he exclaims: "That building on the right is surely the Ducal Palace, and on the left is the entrance to the Piazzetta."

"That lofty tower is, of course, the Campanile. But where is St. Mark's?"

"It is just behind the Ducal Palace, and invisible from this point."

"And the famous Piazza?"

"That, too, is hidden behind the building on the left, but it is at right angles with the Piazzetta, and lies within the shadow of the Campanile."

As one draws nearer to the spot, how marvelously beautiful it all appears! Now one begins to appreciate the splendor of the Doge's Palace. Above it, like a constellation rising from the sea, glitter the domes of the Cathedral of San

Marco. Presently the long landing-pier and the attractive
Piazzetta are distinctly visible; and, turning one's astonished
vision heavenward, one looks with admiration on the splendid
bell-tower, three hundred and fifty feet in height, its pointed
summit piercing the light clouds and its aerial balcony hung
like a gilded cage against the sky. The traveler who beholds
these scenes may have had many delightful moments in his life,
but that in which he looks for the first time upon this glorious
combination of the historic and the beautiful can hardly be
surpassed. Like the names of the old Venetian nobles, it
should be written in a "Book of Gold."

On the border of the Piazzetta are two stately columns.
On landing, therefore, one naturally gives to them one's first
attention. It is difficult to realize that these granite mono-
liths have been standing here for more than seven hundred

THE EDGE OF THE PIAZZETTA.

years, but such is the fact, as they were erected in the year
1187. They were a portion of the spoils brought back by
the Venetians from the treasure-laden East. Each up-
holds the emblem of a patron saint: one, a statue of St.
Theodore; the other, the famous wingèd lion of St. Mark.

Formerly, on a scaffold reared between these columns, state criminals were put to death — their backs turned toward the land which casts them from her, their faces toward the sea, symbol of eternity. But now the shadows of these ancient shafts fall on a multitude of pleasure-boats, and echo to the voices of the gondoliers. Close by these columns is the Ducal Palace,

THE DOGE'S PALACE.

—that splendid symbol of Venetian glory,— a record of the city's brilliant history preserved in stone. This spot, for more than a thousand years, was the resi-

dence of the Doges. Five palaces preceded this, each in turn having been destroyed by fire. But every time a more magnificent building rose from the ashes of its predecessor. The present structure has been standing for nearly five hundred

SANTA MARIA DELLA SALUTÉ.

years, and from the variety of architectural styles mingled
here from North, South, East and West, Ruskin called it,
"The Central Building of the World."

Around it, on two sides, are long arcades of marble columns, the lower ones adorned with sculptures in relief, the
upper ones ending in graceful circles pierced with quatrefoils.

ALONG THE SHORE.

Above them is the crowning glory of the building,—a beautiful expanse of variegated marble, with intricate designs running diagonally over its surface.   At every corner the twisted
column of Byzantine architecture is observed, and on the
border of the roof a fringe of pinnacles and pointed arches
cuts its keen silhouette against the sky.   The lower columns
seem perhaps a trifle short, but this is because the building
has gradually settled toward the sea, as if unable to support
the burden of its years and memories.

By day this palace is superbly beautiful; but, in the
evening, when illumined by the moon, or flooded with electric

light, it is, perhaps, the most imposing structure in the whole of Europe. At such a time it looks like an immense sarcophagus of precious stone, in which the glories of old Venice lie entombed. The colonnades around the Ducal

A CORNER OF THE DUCAL PALACE — THE JUDGMENT OF SOLOMON.

Palace give perfect shelter from the sun or rain, and hundreds stroll here through the day, having the somber palace on the one side, and, on the other, all the gaiety of the Grand Canal. But in the evening, when the adjoining St. Mark's Square is thronged with promenaders, and music floats upon the air, the arcade is to the Piazza what a conservatory is to a ball-room. Lovers invariably find such places, for not even the moonbeams can penetrate these shadows. At such a time the promenades seem shadowy lanes of love conducting from the gay Piazza to the waiting gondola.

To know the past of the Ducal Palace thoroughly would be to know the entire history of Venice, from its transcendent glories to its darkest crimes. For this was not alone the residence of the Doges; it was at different epochs the Senate-House, the Court of Justice, a prison, and even a place of execution. Fronting upon the courtyard, just beneath the roof, the tourist sees some small, round windows. They admit a little light to a few cells, known as the Piombi, or Leads, because they were located just beneath the lead roof of the palace. In summer the heat in them is almost unendurable. And yet in one of them the Italian patriot and poet, Silvio Pellico, seventy years ago, was kept a wretched captive, and he has related the sad story of his sufferings in his famous book, *Le mie Prigioni*, or "My Prisons."

A DUCAL PORTAL.

It is but a step from the outer corridors into the courtyard of the palace. Four elegantly decorated marble walls enclose this, and one instinctively looks up to see the splendid robes of Senators light up the sculptured colonnades, and the rich toilettes of the Venetian ladies trail upon the marble stairways. But no! This square, whose walls have echoed to the footsteps of the Doges, now guards a solemn silence. In its pathetic, voiceless beauty, it is perhaps the saddest spot in Venice.

Two beautiful bronze well-curbs glitter in the foreground; but though the wells which they enclose contain good water, almost no life surrounds them, and to the modern visitor they now

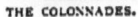

THE COLONNADES.

A WELL-CURB.

resemble gorgeous jewel-caskets, which years ago were rifled of their precious gems.

Beyond these, one observes a marble staircase leading to the second story. It is imposing when one stands before it. Above it frowns the winged lion of St. Mark, as if to challenge all who dare set foot upon these steps. Stationed like sentinels to the right and left are two colossal statues representing Mars and Neptune, which have indeed given the name, "The Giants' Staircase," to this thoroughfare of marble. Their stony silence is almost oppressive. Think of

THE COURTYARD OF THE DOGES.

the splendid pageants and historic scenes which they have looked upon, but which their unimpassioned lips will ne'er describe! Between these figures, on the topmost stair, amid a scene of splendor which even the greatest of Venetian artists could only faintly represent, the Doges

THE GIANTS' STEPS.

were inaugurated into sovereignty. Here they pronounced their solemn oath of office; and one of them, Marino Faliero, having betrayed his trust, was here beheaded for his crime. It will be remembered that Byron's tragedy of Marino Faliero closes with the line:

"The gory head rolls down the Giants' Steps."

A LANDING NEAR THE DUCAL PALACE.

When one has passed these marble giants and entered the
state apartments of the palace, despite the intimation given
by the outer walls, one is astonished at the splendor here
revealed. As the bright sunlight falls on the mosaic pavement, it is easy to imagine that   one is
walking on a beach whose
glittering sands are
grains of gold. The
roof and walls are
covered with enor-
mous masterpieces
set in golden frames.
All of them have
one theme—the glori-

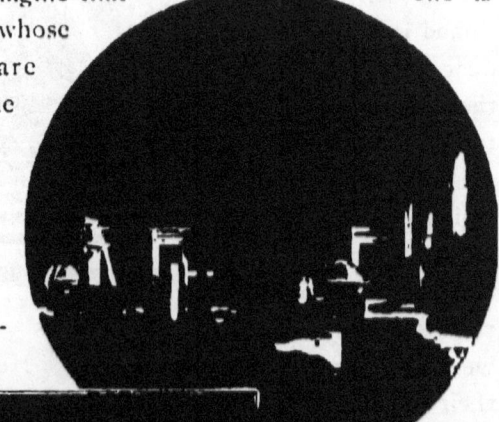

APARTMENTS IN THE
DOGE'S PALACE.

fication of Ven-
ice. One of
them, finished
by Tintoretto
when he was
more than three
score years and
ten, is seventy feet in length, and is the largest painting known
to art. One trembles to think what fire could accomplish
here in a single night, not only in this Ducal Palace, but in
the equally marvelous buildings which adjoin it; for they
could never be reproduced. They are unique in the world.

Each of these gold-enameled halls is like a gorgeous vase,
in which are blooming fadelessly the flowers of Venetian history. What scenes have been enacted here, when on these

THE COURTYARD OF THE DUCAL PALACE.

benches sat the Council-
ors of the Republic wear-
ing their scarlet robes!
Upon their votes depend-
ed life and death; and
here the die was cast for
peace or war. Close by
the door was placed a lion's
head of marble, into the
mouth of which (the famous
Bocca di Lione) secret denun-
ciations were cast. These
were examined by the Council
of Ten, all of whose acts were
shrouded in profoundest secrecy;
and such at last was their despotic

STATUE OF COLLEONI — A VENETIAN
GENERAL.

power that even the Doge himself came to be nothing but
the slave and mouthpiece of that group of tyrants, and was
as little safe from them as those whose sentences he automat-
ically signed.

While standing here, there naturally presents itself to
one's imagination a scene in the old days when, as the Doge
descended from his palace,
he met some lowly suppliant
presenting to him an appeal
for mercy. Ah, what a
glorious age was that for
Venice!—when her victori-
ous flag rolled out its purple
folds over the richest islands
of the Mediterranean and
the Adriatic; when she possessed the largest armory
and the most extensive

THE WINGED LION.

dock-yards in the world (in which ten thousand beams of oak were always ready for the construction of new ships); when she could boast of having the first bank of deposit ever founded in Europe; when (Rome excepted) she was the first to print books in Italy; and when she sold in St. Mark's

THE GOLDEN AGE OF VENICE.

Square the first newspaper ever known to the world, demanding for it a little coin called *gazetta*, which has given us the word "gazette."

Recalling these Venetian exploits, I stood one evening in one of the most delightful places in all Venice,—the upper balcony of the Ducal Palace. Lingering here and looking out between the sculptured columns toward the island of San Giorgio, I thought of the old times when every year, upon Ascension Day, the Doge descended from this balcony and stepped upon a barge adorned with canopies of gold and velvet, and with a deck inlaid with ebony and mother-of-pearl. Then, to the sound of martial music, that splendid vessel swept out toward the sea, propelled by eighty gilded oars; till, finally, amidst the roar of cannon and the shouts of the assembled populace, the Doge cast into the blue waves a

ISLAND OF SAN GIORGIO.

ring of gold, exclaiming solemnly: "We wed-thee, O Sea, with this ring, emblem of our rightful and perpetual dominion."

But there was another side to this magnificent picture, which dimmed the splendor of Venetian palaces. For just behind the residence of the Doges, suspended over the canal, —"a palace and a prison on each hand,"—is one of the best known structures in the world,— the Bridge of Sighs. This is indeed a sad memorial of tyranny. True, recent scoffers at sentiment sneer at the associations of this bridge, and one has even called it a "pathetic swindle." But, whether or not the prisoners of Venice breathed through these grated windows a last sigh, as they relinquished life and liberty, certain it is that in the building on the right, far down below the water's edge, are some of the most horrible dungeons that

human cruelty has ever designed; and any visitor to Venice may cross this bridge and grope his way down moldering flights of stone steps to behold them.

All who have done so will recollect those fetid cells, slimy with dampness, shrouded in darkness, and stifling from the ex-

A VENETIAN FISHER BOY.

hausted air which filters to them through the narrow corridors. They will remember the iron grating through which was passed the scanty food that for a time prolonged the prisoner's life; the grooves of the old guillotine, by means of which, after excruciating torture, he was put to death; and then the narrow opening through which the body was removed at night and rowed out to a distant spot, where it was death to cast a net. Here, unillumined even by a torch, it sank, freighted with heavy stones, into the sea, whose gloomy depths will guard all secrets hidden in its breast until its waters shall give up their dead.

Connected with the Ducal residence is the world-renowned St. Mark's Cathedral. The old

BRIDGE OF SIGHS.

Venetians built not only palaces for men; they made their shrines to God palatial. I looked on this one with bewilderment. There is no structure like it in the world. Its bulbous

domes and minaret-like belfries remind one of the Orient. It
seems more like a Mohammedan than a Christian temple.
If the phrase be permitted, it is a kind of Christian mosque.
The truth is, the Venetians brought back from their victories
in the East ideas of Oriental architecture which had pleased

ST. MARK'S CATHEDRAL.

them, and were thus able to produce a wonderful blending of
Moorish, Arabic, and Gothic art.

What a façade is this! Here, massed in serried ranks, are
scores of variously colored marble columns, each one a mono-
lith, and all possessing an eventful history. Some are from
Ephesus, others from Smyrna, while others still are from Constantinople, and more than one even from Jerusalem. On
one, the hand of Cleopatra may have rested; another may
have cast its shadow on St. Paul; a third may have been
looked upon by Jesus. St. Mark's is the treasure-house of

THE BRONZE HORSES.

Venice, — a place of pride as well as of prayer. Here was heaped up the booty which she gained from her repeated conquests. The Doge's Palace was the brain of Venice; the Grand Piazza was its heart; but this Cathedral was its soul.

The work of beautifying this old church was carried on enthusiastically for five hundred years. Each generation tried to outdo all that had preceded it. Again and again Venetian fleets swept proudly up the Adriatic, laden with spoils destined for this glorious shrine. *Viva San Marco!* was the watchword alike of her armies and her navies; and when the captains of Venetian fleets came homeward from the Orient, the first inquiry put to them was this: "What new and splendid offering bring you for San Marco?" The dust of ages, therefore, may have

THE PORTAL OF ST. MARK'S.

gathered on this building, but it is, at least, the dust of gold. Its domes and spires glisten with the yellow luster. It even gilds the four bronze horses which surmount its portal. These are among the most interesting statues in the world. We know not who the sculptor was that gave them their apparent life; but it is certain that they were

CORNER OF THE CATHEDRAL.

carried to Rome and there attached to Nero's golden chariot. In the fourth century after Christ the emperor Constantine, when he transferred the seat of empire from the Tiber to the Bosphorus, took them to Constantinople, where for nine hundred years they proudly stood beside the Golden Horn. Then, when that capital was plundered by the Venetians, they were brought hither, and for five hundred years they adorned the entrance to St. Mark's. Even here their travels had not ended; for, a century ago, Napoleon, when conqueror of Italy, caused them to be conveyed to Paris, where, in the shadow of the Tuileries, they watched the triumph of the modern Cæsar. But after Waterloo,

A VENETIAN LANE.

Venice once more claimed them for her own.

It is an impressive moment when one passes beneath these gilded steeds and enters the interior of the cathedral. A twilight gloom pervades it, well suited to its age and the mysterious origin of all it contains. The walls and roof are so profusely covered with mosaics and precious marbles that it is easy to understand why St. Mark's has been called the "Church of Gold," and likened to a cavern hung with stalactites of precious stones. Some of these ornaments are of pagan origin; others have come from Christian shrines. All, however, have had to pay their contribution to St. Mark's. Thus Santa Sophia at Constantinople, though still a Christian church and dedicated to the Saviour, was plundered to embellish the Venetian shrine named after His apostle. Hence, it is the literal truth that, overflowing with the spoils of other cities and sanctuaries, St. Mark's is a magnificent repository of booty — a veritable den of thieves. In the most prominent position in the church is the receptacle

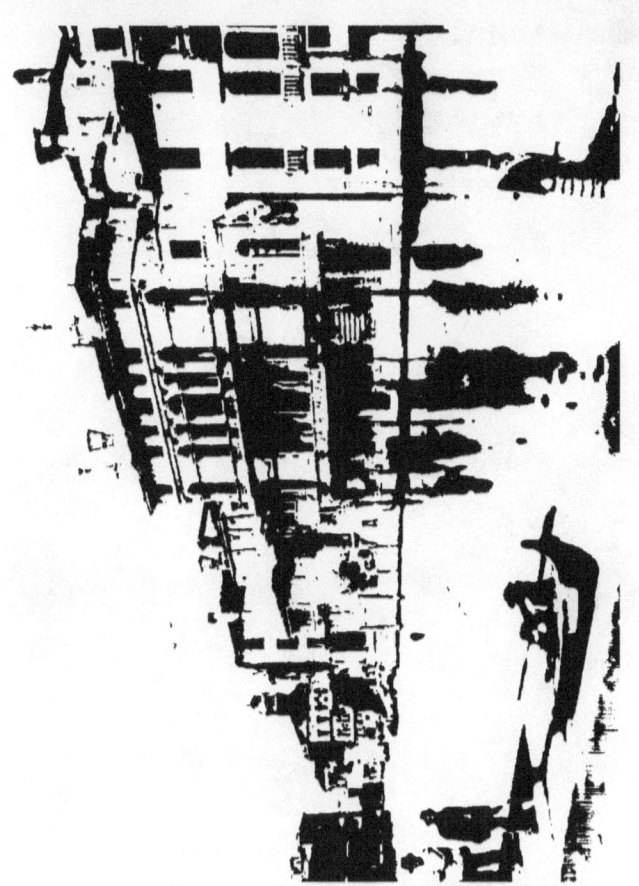

guarded by the statues of the twelve apostles, where is kept, as the most precious of its treasures, the body of St. Mark. On one side is the pulpit from which the old Doge, Dandolo, when ninety-three years of age, urged his people to undertake the fourth crusade.

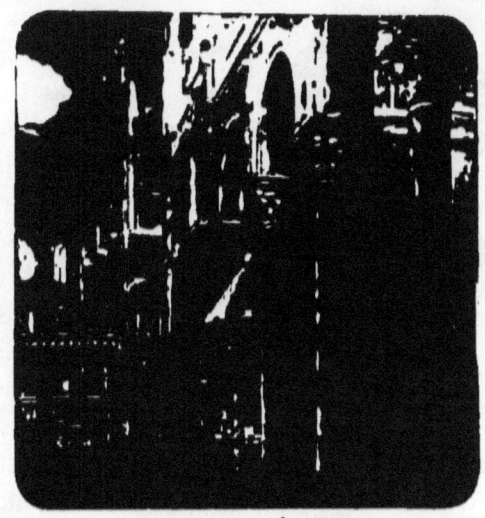

INTERIOR OF ST. MARK'S CATHEDRAL.

"Men of Venice!" he exclaimed, "I am old and weak, and I need rest, but I will go with you to rescue from the infidel the Holy Sepulchre, and I will be victorious or lose my life." Hearing these words, the assembled people made these walls resound with the cry: "So be it! Lead us on! For God's sake go with us!" Then the old Doge descended from the pulpit, and standing on the steps between the jasper columns, received the badge of the Crusaders, the

THE STATUES OF THE APOSTLES.

A TYPE OF GONDOLIER.

Cross of Christ, a miniature reproduction of the colossal crucifix, which glittered then, as it still gleams to-day, above the place on which he stood.

On leaving this marvelous structure, one steps directly into the adjoining St. Mark's Square. If it be the hour of siesta, it will appear deserted. Yet this has been for centuries the Forum of Venetian life; the favorite place for her festivities; the beautiful, historic stage on which have been enacted most of the scenes connected with her glorious past. Around it are fine marble structures, which even now are used for offices of State. Within these long arcades are the most attractive shops in Venice, and, were there only a garden in the centre, the place would remind one of the Palais Royal at Paris, which was, in fact, built in imitation of this square.

To-day the popularity of the Parisian square is waning, since many of its gorgeous shops have migrated to the Rue de la Paix. But owing to its situation, the attractiveness of the Venetian court can hardly be diminished. While Venice lasts, its glory must remain undimmed by Time.

On summer evenings, when the city wakes to life and music, the famous square bursts into the gaiety of a ball-room, and is the

A FISHERMAN.

favorite rendezvous of all lovers and pleasure-seekers, whether natives or foreigners. Here, several times a week, fine military music floats upon the air, and hundreds of men and women stroll along these marble blocks, which in the moon-

THE PIAZZA DI SAN MARCO.

light seem as white as snow. Others, meantime, are seated beneath the neighboring arches, sipping coffee or sherbet, laughing and talking in the soft Venetian dialect, and, like the Japanese, seeming to appreciate the mere joy of living, an art which many of us, alas, have lost.

One pretty feature of this historic area is its pigeons. Their homes are in the marble arches of the adjoining buildings; and shortly after midday, every afternoon, they suddenly appear in great numbers; now rising in a pretty cloud of fluttering wings; now grouped together like an undulating wave of eider-down. Foreigners, in particular, love to

FEEDING THE PIGEONS.

feed them; and in return for the kindness they receive, the pigeons at times alight upon the shoulders of a stranger or courageously pick up crumbs from outstretched hands. It is not strange that Venice should guard these birds so tenderly. Six centuries ago, when the Venetians were blockading the island of Candia, the Doge's officers observed that pigeons frequently flew above their heads. Suspecting something, they contrived to shoot a few, and each was found to have beneath its wing a message to the enemy. Acting on information thus acquired, the Venetian admiral made his attack at once and captured the island in twelve hours. The carrier-pigeons which they found there were therefore taken home to Venice and treated with the utmost kindness, and their descendants have ever since been favorites of the people.

On walking from the Piazza toward the Grand Canal, one always finds at the extremity of the Piazzetta a line of waiting gondolas. At once a shower of soft Italian syllables falls musically on the air: "Una gondola, Signore! Commanda una gondola; Una barca, Signore; Una bellissima barca;

A VENETIAN COURTYARD.

Vuol' andare? Eccomi pronto!'' The speakers are Venetian
coachmen, and the contrast is a startling one between the
liquid vowels of their speech and the rasping cries of our
American drivers: ''Want a cow-pay, lady?'' ''Want a
kerridge?'' ''Want a hack—hack—hack?'' As for the gondoliers themselves, how picturesque they look with their white
suits and colored scarfs! Who can resist the impulse to enter
one of these pretty barges and give oneself to the enjoyment
of the hour?

Few things are more delightful than floating here in a
gondola after the heat of a summer day. We say summer,
for Venice should, if possible, be always visited in warm
weather—the healthiest season here. Then only can one
thoroughly enjoy its outdoor life. However sultry it may be
on land, in Venice it is reasonably cool, and the broad bosom of

the Adriatic, as it swells
and falls, breathes
through the streets of
Venice the delicious
freshness of the sea.
At such a time, to idly
float upon this beauti-
ful expanse, dreaming
of art and history (per-
chance of love), through
the sweet, tranquil
hours which bear upon
their noiseless wings
the hint of a repose still
held in the unfolded
hands of Night,—that
is happiness,—that is
rest! At such a time
one loves to call to

WAITING GONDOLAS.

mind the scenes which must have often taken place upon the surface of this siren sea, when Venice had no less than thirty thousand gondolas, of which at least one-third were richly decorated, and vied with one another in their gilded draperies and carvings. To such an extent, indeed, did reckless competition in them go, that the Doge finally issued a decree that they should thenceforth have black awnings only. Since then Venetian gondolas have been prosaic in appearance, though their dark awnings have increased the opportunities for crime or intrigue, and they have often been the rendezvous of hate or love,— ideal vehicles for murder or elopement.

IN A GONDOLA.

"In Venice Tasso's echoes are no more,
And silent rows the songless gondolier:
Her palaces are crumbling to the shore,
And music meets not always now the ear:
Those days are gone — but Beauty still is here.
States fall, arts fade,— but Nature doth not die,
Nor yet forget how Venice once was dear,
The pleasant place of all festivity,
The revel of the earth, the masque of Italy!"

To the lover of the beautiful in Nature the most enchanting characteristic of this City of the Sea is its sunset glow. Italian sunsets are all beautiful; but those of Venice are the loveliest of all. Their softness, brilliancy and splendor cannot be described. The last which I beheld here, on a night

in June, surpassed all others I had ever seen. The shadows
were falling to the eastward; the hush of night was stealing
on the world. The cares of life seemed disappearing down
the radiant west together with the God of Day. Between us
and the setting sun there seemed to fall a shower of powdered

LIKE A BEAUTIFUL MIRAGE.

gold. The entire city was pervaded by a golden light, which
yet was perfectly transparent, like the purest ether.

As we drew nearer to the Grand Canal the scene grew even
more enchanting. In the refulgent light the city lay before
us like a beautiful mirage, enthroned upon a golden bank
between two seas,—the ocean and the sky. Her streets
seemed filled with liquid sunshine. The steps of her patrician
palaces appeared entangled in the meshes of a golden net.
The neighboring islands looked like jeweled wreckage floating
from a barge of gold. The whole effect was that of a poem
without words, illustrated by Titian, and having for a soft

accompaniment the ripple of the radiant waves. I have seen many impressive sights in many climes; but for triumphant beauty, crystallized in stone and glorified by the setting sun, I can recall no scene more matchless in its loveliness than that which I enjoyed, when, on this richly-tinted sea, I watched the Bride and Sovereign of the Adriatic pass to the curtained chamber of the night enveloped in a veil of gold.

IN VENICE AT SUNSET.

www.ingramcontent.com/pod-product-compliance
Lightning Source LLC
Chambersburg PA
CBHW031336070726
47496CB00017B/1133